ANICA MROSE RISSI

NOBODY KNOWS BUT YOU

Quill Tree Books
An Imprint of HarperCollinsPublishers

Quill Tree Books is an imprint of HarperCollins Publishers.

Library of Congress Control Number: 2020933535
ISBN 978-0-06-268531-5

Typography by Molly Fehr
20 21 22 23 24   PC/LSCH   10 9 8 7 6 5 4 3 2 1

❖

First Edition

For Stephanie "Jimmy" Su,
wherever you might be

August 23

Dear Lainie,

I swore to you we would always keep in touch, that I'd call and text and visit and write, so here goes, though neither of us could have imagined it would be quite like this. I'll delete this as soon as it's written, of course. Destroying the evidence, just like you taught me, haha. Remember that? The first night we snuck out. You set your alarm on vibrate and promised to wake me at 12:13 a.m., but I didn't sleep while I waited. I lay frozen after lights-out, barely breathing, my heart pounding so loudly I was sure it would wake our whole cabin, if not the entire camp. Each second took minutes, millennia, to squeak past, and my brain was freaking out the whole time, spinning cartwheels around the trouble we'd be in when we got caught.

I rehearsed a billion excuses, but soon my stomach ached for real as I imagined the shrug you might give before slipping out the screen door into the night, leaving me behind and forgotten—my shot at being your friend, partner in crime, or anything else, blown completely. I still didn't know why you'd invited me along in the first place. It was only the third day of camp and we'd barely spoken four words. (I'd barely said that much to anyone.) The invitation felt random, but also—don't laugh—it felt a lot like fate. Like a chance to change my fate.

But I couldn't do it. I'm a rule-follower at heart, not a rebel like you. I was going to chicken out.

Just when time had slowed so much it was basically standing still, it skipped forward, too fast, and before I knew it, you were climbing down from the top bunk, swift and silent, like a cat. Without moving a hand, you pulled me with you. I forgot my excuses and the fear dropped away as you walked out the door and I followed close behind, barely believing the person who, in that moment, at your invitation, I'd become.

It was freaking exhilarating.

You led the way past the cabins, down the hill toward the lake. A twig beneath my feet cracked like thunder, but it didn't wake the counselors or the dead. (Okay, I winced when I just wrote that, the word *dead*. It made my stomach twist so hard, I thought I might vom, but then I heard your laugh in my head—you always laughed in terrible moments like this—and now I want to puke and cry and laugh too, all at once. Picturing that makes the *you* in my head crack up harder, which is all I want: to be laughing at something completely inappropriate with you again. So now I'm sitting here grinning through tears like a snotty mess, and I miss you so fucking much, can I just say that?)

How weird is it to think that before this summer, I never used to curse? You, my friend, were a terrible influence.

(Now the *you* in my head is rolling her eyes and nudging me. "Ahem. You were telling a story?")

Right. I'll continue.

I followed you to the lake, out onto the dock, and we sat cross-legged on the cool wooden planks while the waves lapped softly below us. You leaned back on your hands, tilted your face up to the stars, and the look of total peace that came across it made me wonder

August 22, 10:58 p.m.

hey
I miss you
you don't even know how much
I wish I could tell you everything
I wish I could tell you I'm sorry

for all of it

all of it except you and me

Sorry but I think you have the wrong number

fuck you for not being her

September 3
Channel 5 News

"Tragic accident or deadly revenge?

"Sources from within the state prosecutor's office say the DA is close to filing charges against a teenage suspect in the sensational case that has shocked and gripped viewers across the region since the fateful night three weeks ago that left one sixteen-year-old summer camper dead and another under suspicion of murder.

"Michael Desir, an attorney for the teen who is at the center of the ongoing police investigation, maintains his client's innocence, even as prosecutor Marsha Davis is expected to bring charges within the week. Despite few official facts having been released in the case, rumors and speculation run rampant online, fueled by social media posts from other campers and their parents and counselors. Some have suggested that the delays in pressing charges could indicate major weaknesses in the state's attempt to build a case proving the camper's untimely death was a passion-fueled crime, not a tragic accident.

"The prosecutor's office would not comment on whether the teenage suspect will be charged as a minor or—given the severity of the alleged crime—as an adult."

NOBODY KNOWS BUT YOU

what troubles had come before. You smiled at the universe like you owned it, then you turned that smile toward me. "Isn't this the best thing you've ever done?" you asked, already sure of the answer.

"I was so nervous," I admitted. "I've never straight-up broken the rules before. I don't think I'm cut out for a life of crime."

You shook your head. "You were born for this. You're a ninja. A fox. A motherfucking stealth pro." I couldn't tell if you were teasing or serious or both, but a giddiness spread through my chest. A giggle escaped, and you were laughing too, silently, your shoulders shaking and your lips pressed tight to hold it in.

The dock rocked beneath our butts and the smell of lake water filled my head, and I asked, "Do fishes sleep?" and you released an epic snort and laughed so hard you almost fell over.

"You're so random," you said when you'd caught your breath. It felt like the best compliment ever.

Your face got serious and you reached into your pocket, pulled something out, and announced, "I brought contraband."

I'd been preparing for this moment since the day in fourth grade when Officer Dunkel warned us about the dangers of peer pressure, but no one had ever offered me cigarettes or drugs before. (I *told* you I lived a sheltered existence.) I was polite but firm. "No, thank you. I don't smoke."

"What?" You blinked, then choked on another laugh. "Oh my god. Raaaaaaaandommmmm," you sang, and as you opened your hand further I saw what lay inside: two sticks of gum. The white wrappers shone in the moonlight. So did your grin.

"I thought it was cigarettes. Or, like, pot," I explained. "It looked

5

like a joint in the dark."

You shook your head. "Okay, Randy." I wasn't even embarrassed, just thrilled you'd given me a nickname. I accepted the gum and folded it into my mouth, and you produced a lighter from your hoodie. You flicked it on and your eyes danced with fire. "The first rule of crime is: Always Destroy the Evidence," you said solemnly. You held your wrapper to the flame and we watched it burn. The ashes blew over the water and disappeared, and you handed the lighter to me.

If I could turn back time, give us a chance to start over—figure out how to change what happened to you in the end—which moment would I send us back to? I think about this a lot. I know it's a pointless question. I'm not going to stumble across a time machine or wake up to a second-chance summer. But the answer still seems important, like I need to figure it out. Like if I can pinpoint the moment where things went so wrong, I might rewrite the terrible ending.

Dr. Rita, the shrink my parents are pushing me off on so they won't have to help me through this themselves, says I can't blame myself for what happened, and I don't. I blame Jackson. Duh.

And sometimes, a little bit, in the worst moments, I blame you, or at least wonder how I could have convinced you. I know it's not my fault, any of what happened with you and him, but that doesn't stop my brain or heart from cycling through the what-ifs. And there are a lot of those.

Here's a big one: What if on that last night, the night of the accident, when you climbed down from your bunk—stepping left to avoid the spot on the middle rung that creaked—what if I hadn't held still and pretended to be asleep? What if I'd gotten out of bed, followed you outside, and insisted on tagging along like the third wheel I'd sometimes become? Would you have sent me away? Would Jackson? Would it have changed anything? Or everything? Or nothing?

It hurts to think about. It hurts to imagine how things might be different now, the million-and-one ways. I could be writing you messages you'd actually read and reply to. Driving up to see you on weekends. Making you laugh again for real.

But I didn't. You aren't. You won't.

You never will.

I hate this so much and I can't even tell you.

I miss you more than you'll ever know.

Love,
Kayla

August 27

Dear Lainie,

I didn't want to go to Camp Cavanick. I wanted to stay home and sleep late, read books, enjoy air conditioning, and avoid bugs and "fun" and other humans. But my parents wouldn't tolerate "another summer of you moping around the house" and I didn't get into the science camp that was my first choice of torture. (Which is fair—I suck at science. Or rather, I'm as average at science as I am at everything else, no matter how hard my parents refuse to accept that. I'm sixteen years old and have shown zero signs of excelling at anything, but Adele and Peter still seem to be awaiting my acceptance from Hogwarts, or for my hidden superpowers to suddenly reveal themselves at the dinner table, proving I'm as extraordinary as everyone else in this family, not the dud of the bunch I've so far turned out to be. Not because they see any particular aptitude in me, but because they are so accomplished and high-achieving, it's unfathomable that one of their children would turn out to be *normal*. Poor them. At least they've got my brother upholding the family standard of excellence—at Swarthmore, no less. La-di-da.)

I don't love or excel at science, but I figured at least science camp would be chock-full of nerds. It wouldn't matter if I was socially awkward or kind of a loner, because if anything, that would help me fit in.

But alas: I got rejected, even from reject camp. So Adele enrolled me at Camp Cavanick ("A Summer of Fun. A Lifetime of Memories. Exclusively for Teens!") without my permission (though she swore she discussed it with me first), and while they didn't exactly drag me there kicking and screaming—I do have *some* dignity— I made everyone as miserable as possible in the weeks leading up to my departure, lest they think they had won and there was any chance I might enjoy myself even slightly. Which of course made them all the more relieved to be dropping me off in the middle of nowhere for eight weeks of being blissfully free of me. I would feel bad about how I acted, but it's my job as a teenager to help them detach and almost hate me, so when it's time for me to fly the nest, they won't feel too hopeless and sad. My awful behavior is actually deeply altruistic, see? YOU'RE WELCOME, PARENTS. Haha.

But I guess the joke was on me. I steeled myself for the worst and loneliest summer of my life (being alone with other people around is so much worse than being *alone* alone—I'm never lonely by myself, or at least I wasn't before now), and instead I met you. The best thing that ever happened to me.

Is it really better to have loved and lost than never to have loved at all?

I assumed it was Shakespeare who wrote that, but I just googled to check and turns out it was Alfred Lord Tennyson. "'Tis better to have loved and lost Shakespeare" is one of the top suggested auto-fills, though, so I must not be the only one who thought that. Man, Shakespeare gets the credit for everything, doesn't he. All the other dead writers must hate him.

I feel like before I met you, I wasn't even fully myself. I was a larva. A plain, unremarkable caterpillar that, in your presence, changed into a beauuuuuuutiful butterfly. It's like you saw the very best version of me, and by seeing it, you helped me become it.

I don't even know who I was before I became your best friend. I don't know who I am now without you. I'm sure this new reality will sink in eventually, but right now it doesn't compute. And I don't want it to. "Loved and lost" or "Never loved at all" are shitty options. 'Tis better to have loved and stayed best friends forever. *That's* what I wanted for you and me.

Ugh, I am so sick of crying over you. Dammit. How does someone recover from the loss of their very best friend?

No, really: HOW???

Cue Dr. Rita voice: *It takes time to process and absorb, let alone move past, a significant trauma like this. You're still in shock, and that's okay. You've got many stages of grief to go through. You might not feel truly okay and like yourself for quite some time— and that's all right too.*

Well, it's not all right with me.

She can take her bloody trauma talk and shove it.

(Get it? *Bloody?* Hahahahahahahahahaha *sob*)

Why am I still trying to make you laugh? Old habits die hard, I guess.

(*Die! Ba-dum-ching!*)

Seriously, folks, I'll be here all night.

I will, though. I can't sleep because I'm haunted by the ghosts of my past, who insist on replaying the highlight reel on endless loop. It's *It's a Wonderful Life* meets *I Know What You Did Last Summer.* Grab some popcorn and enjoy the show.

I definitely got funnier being friends with you, since it was basically my daily mission to make you crack up. I was good at it. I loved how your lips twitched whenever I made some goofy, random remark. ("What's in it?" "Artichoke." "Ah! A pirate's favorite vegetable.") Loved how the smallest things grew into inside jokes we ping-ponged back and forth for as long as humanly possible. ("Aye, matey, aside from Swiss charrrrrrd." "Who told ye that, Old Salt?" "Farrrrmer Jack." "That landlubber." "Replace him with an arrrrrrdvarrrrk!" "Send him to the Arrrrrrrrctic!" "Farrrrrr as the carrrrrrrrr will go.") Loved how other people looked at us when we really got going: part amused, part envious, part admiring, part confused. How they laughed along like they were in on our jokes, but never fully got them. ("Isn't that right, John?" "That's right, John.") How they wished they could be part of us. We didn't exclude them—we weren't bitches—but I didn't need anyone but you, you didn't need anyone but me, and most people knew that.

Okay, that's not true. You definitely needed other people. You needed an audience.

You reeled people in, then held them at arm's length, never letting them get truly close. But me, you let in. I loved the real you, flaws and all.

I wish that could have been enough for you.

I know exactly how you would react to this. I can picture you so clearly, propping your chin on both hands, blinking your eyes wide, and saying, "Tell me more, Dr. Randy," your voice the kind of mock serious that would make me toss a pillow at you if I had one. But I'm the daughter of not one but *two* child psychologists. It's in my blood to psychoanalyze—or to be psycho, take your pick.

But yeah. No one else truly gets our sense of humor, which leaves me kind of screwed, if you think about it. I spent all summer perfecting my act for an audience of one, and that audience has left the theater.

Have I mentioned that I miss you?

You probably remember what I told you about the first (and only other) time I went to camp, the summer before fifth grade. How the girls in my cabin were intimidating and cliquey, and I was always on the edge of what was happening, never in on the fun or the jokes, but I didn't understand how outside of it I was, or that they all hated me, until the night they hung Ollie.

The week before camp, I thought long and hard about which of my treasured stuffed animals should accompany me. I would miss each one that didn't make the cut, but it seemed important to only bring one, so as not to seem too babyish, and I felt certain the right choice would make me seem cool. It couldn't be a teddy bear or anything too well loved or too new-looking. It should be something quirky and interesting, the kind of companion that would make *me* seem interesting. One pretty enough that the others would secretly want it, but offbeat enough that it would look almost ironic propped against the pillow on my bunk. (Yes, this whole thing makes me cringe now too. I was a total dork.)

Scruffy, long-necked Ollie the baby ostrich won out. She was one of my sweetest animal friends—scrappy and a little awkward, with a trusting but intelligent face. I loved her puffy gray body and cute little beak, and her fuzzy white head felt soft beneath my chin when we cuddled in the dark.

None of the other girls in my cabin brought stuffed animals, or if they did, they kept them hidden in their duffel bags. The cooler, more sophisticated girls brought makeup kits: palettes with eye shadow in a hundred shades; plastic cases filled with polishes, powders, pencils, creams, and brushes. They sat on one another's bunks and did each other's faces, styled each other's hair. Rubbed perfume samples on wrists they held out for sniffs and approval.

I studied the ways they talked and moved, in case I got a chance to be one of them.

I was never invited to the makeover parties, though I was present, just a bunk or two away. I sat, cross-legged, with a book on my lap, trying to look available but not desperate. Interruptible, but not unoccupied. But just like at school, I was an outcast. Invisible. Irrelevant. Unremarkable and ignored.

But one day, one of the girls noticed Ollie and asked me about her. She was curious and complimentary, and other kids gathered around us and cooed over how cute Ollie was. I even let a few of them hold her. My heart beat double-speed the whole time, I was so eager and thrilled to be finally making friends.

The giant bell they used to signal mealtimes and stuff clanged, and we left for afternoon activities. I dipped long wicks into containers of hot wax—lowering them in slowly, lifting them back out. Waiting, then dipping again. I thought about how making candles was like making friends: slow at first—kind of monotonous, even—and requiring patience through the endless early stages. But layer by layer, you could build something solid. My persistence was finally paying off. Maybe that night I'd be invited to join the makeovers.

Maybe tomorrow I'd be included in their games.

When I went back to the cabin to grab a sweatshirt before dinner, the girl who'd asked about Ollie was there. She and her friend erupted in giggles and I smiled back full-faced before I saw what they—or someone—had done. Hanging from the rafters, a ratty shoelace around her neck, was Ollie. The sign taped to her chest said "DEAD BIRD" in block letters. Her big feet and little wings flopped above me.

Pain squeezed my heart and I wanted to scale the bunks and save her, but the girls' expectant gazes froze me in place. I couldn't show them my devastation. I wouldn't give them what they craved.

I tried to keep my expression unchanged. "Oh!" I said. "Haha. So funny."

Uncertainty flickered in their faces, or maybe it was disappointment. "You're not mad?"

"No!" I insisted. "That's hilarious. Who did it?"

They swore they didn't know but agreed it was genius, and I kept my smile plastered on and followed them to the mess hall, leaving Ollie where she was. Inside I was screaming. I wanted to claw those girls' eyes out, make them wail the way I wished I could be wailing. I wanted to rescue Ollie, cradle her in my arms, and take her someplace safe from this humiliation and awfulness. But I didn't. I couldn't.

I deserted her. I was a traitor to the only friend I had.

When we returned to the cabin that night, Ollie was no longer dangling from the rafters. The counselor who'd cut her down returned her to me with some sharp words about "the kind of humor that doesn't belong at Camp Paddywack," as if *I* had done that horrible thing to my own fuzzy friend and thought it was *funny*. I didn't correct her. I accepted Ollie back, removed the remnants of her noose, and tucked us deep inside my sleeping bag, where I wished I could stay hidden forever, or at least until the end of camp.

I told Dr. Rita about Ollie in our session yesterday and she waited with that I'm-really-listening face therapists get, then asked, "How did that make you feel?" I burst into tears, not because of the mean girls and Ollie and my failure as her protector and friend, but because when I told *you* this same story, you didn't ask how I felt—you knew, immediately, without needing to be told. You exhaled out your nose like a bull blowing smoke, and said, "Fuck those girls. They're not worthy to pet the soft tufts of Ollie's behind," so viciously that the story suddenly seemed funny—not like something shameful I had suffered alone, but a slight you rebuffed on my behalf, a pathetic attempt by those girls to deflate me. An experience we were in on together.

You asked me what Ollie was doing this summer, and I admitted I'd left her propped on my bed with a copy of *Anne of Green Gables*. You nodded and said, "Good. She deserves some nice R and R." Then we debated *Anne of Green Gables* versus *Emily of New Moon*, Nancy Drew versus Cam Jansen versus Charlotte Holmes versus Harriet the Spy, and Paddington Bear versus Corduroy (a standoff promptly won by Winnie the Pooh).

I've never had a friend who *gets* me like you do. Did.

But I didn't want to go into that again with Dr. Rita, so I let her think I was crying over the mean girls and Ollie—over what happened way back when, instead of over you. I didn't mention I had ever even told you that story. Because it's starting to feel like the more I talk about you, the less anyone understands, and the further I get from you, the *real* you, even though you're only two weeks gone. I can't capture you correctly with words or even memories, can't keep you present and real through stories (the way you could make anything real in the telling). I don't want to explain our friendship to other people who weren't in it. I only want to talk about you with *you*. But these letters are as close as I'll get.

There's another kind of candle-making I learned that summer besides the hand-dipping kind. We also used wet sand to form molds that we filled with hot wax—poured it in smooth and fast, then let it cool and harden around the wick. That's the way you and I became friends: swift and sudden, no gradual buildup. Overnight, our friendship solidified, as though by some grand design. We burned hot and bright, and I thought the flame would last forever. Then Jackson snuffed it out.

You were the best thing that ever happened to me. I never dreamed it would end with the worst.

Love,
Kayla

August 14
Channel 5 News

"Developing news we're following closely tonight: Police in Maplewash County are asking parents and campers to remain calm and stay put as they investigate the circumstances of a teenage camper's death that occurred late last night or early this morning at Camp Cavanick on Jaspertown Lake. There has been no official statement from Camp Cavanick administrators to the media as of yet, but concerned parents of the approximately two hundred thirteen-to-seventeen-year-olds at the camp say they were notified at around noon today of the unfathomable tragedy that occurred overnight, only one and a half days before the eight-week session was to end.

"Here's what some parents on the scene, awaiting news from their campers, had to say about it."

"The email said almost nothing. Just that a camper had died but it wasn't our kid, and police and grief counselors were there, and more information would be forthcoming. But nothing has been forthcoming yet; we're just hearing a lot of rumors. The kids are in shock. They're all grieving."

"We got right in the car the minute we got the email. A thing like that happens, you want to make sure your kid is safe—to hold them in your arms and know it's true. Camp phone lines were jammed and most phones don't get good service here; you can only get through on text. So we drove right up, three and a half hours, my wife redialing the whole time, but not until we arrived did we get to talk to her. They don't want us to take them home yet, say it's best for them all to stay put. Well, they don't get to decide what's right for my family, my kid. That's my decision to make as a parent."

"You send your kid off to camp, it's just the last thing you expect. This is so traumatic for the kids—someone they knew, spent all summer with, for a thing like this to happen. I hope the people in charge know good lawyers because I can't be the only one who heard this news and thought, *My kid shows any harm, any damage from this, one hair out of place, and I'll sue.* Just imagine what the parents of the dead kid are thinking. It's every parent's nightmare, I'll tell you that."

"We don't have a lot of information. They say the police are still interviewing everyone and I guess a few kids already gave statements and were cleared to leave and pack up, but they expect to let most of us take our kids home tomorrow. So until then, we're here. We're here for them, and we'll wait."

"But one camper will not be returning home tomorrow, or ever again. Police are still conducting preliminary interviews with any and all individuals who might have relevant information to share, and awaiting results of an autopsy. At this time, they say they are investigating all leads and are unable to yet rule out any possible scenarios for the cause of death, including suicide, tragic accident, or foul play.

"We'll share more details as the story continues."

August 14, 12:14 p.m.

Oh my god, Kayla

We got an email from the camp. What is going on there?

Please tell us you're okay

I'm not ok

Oh, honey. Your dad and I will be there soon.

no

We're coming to get you

don't

mom

I can't leave her

I don't want to go

Camper and Counselor Interviews, Statements, and Posts
August 14–November 24

"Sure, I knew them. Everyone did. Lainie, Kayla, and Jackson were Camp Famous. Everyone knew who they were and what they'd been up to. We were all watching and talking about them, long before anything bad happened."

"Lainie and Kayla were joined at the hip from day one. Got in all sorts of trouble together. I figured they knew each other from before, but I guess they just insta-bonded or whatever. At first I kind of thought *they* were a couple, before Jackson came along."

"Lainie and Kayla were just this *unit*. You would have thought they'd been friends for years, though camp time is like that. One week at camp is like six months in the real world. And at the same time, it flies by so quickly. It's weird. I have friends I was tight with only the last ten days of camp and I know them better than people I've been friends with all of high school. You kind of have to experience it to know about it, but it's true."

"Yeah, Lainie. She and Kayla had this totally codependent relationship. Like . . . what's the thing they talk about in Biology? Where two different organisms have to feed off each other to survive? Symbiosis! They were like that. Inseparable. You'd have thought they were one being, like lichen or some shit . . . at least until Lainie met Jackson and started siphoning off him instead.

"Wait, is it called something different if one of the organisms destroys the other?"

"I feel really bad for Kayla in all this. I mean, that was her best friend. I saw her the day after and she looked completely devastated. We all were, but especially her. She was broken over it, and just . . . lost. And looking back now, I wonder if some part of her saw it coming. If she knew before the rest of us that it wasn't a terrible accident. Based on something she saw, or something Lainie had told her. Or gut instinct. It would be awful, as the best friend, to carry that."

August 31

Dear Lainie,

The second rule of crime is Always Dress to Kill (dark clothing; no flip-flops), but I will not be killing it the first day of school, as I've forgotten how to wear anything besides this one grubby top I've had on for three days and the flannel PJ bottoms I accidentally stole from you (sorry), though I'm guessing you haven't missed them. I still haven't fully unpacked my bags from camp, nor tried on the clothes Adele bought. She knew better than to drag me back-to-school shopping, all things considered. Instead the entire J.Crew catalog has shown up on my doorstep, and I'm too depressed to point out that's her style, not mine. But I'll probably wear it. All that stuff from summer is stained with too many memories. It still smells like the lake.

Flip-flops are verboten at my high school anyway.

I will never forget the way you arched a single eyebrow and shot down the boys with a "Really? *Audible* footwear?" the first time they snuck out with us. It was a miracle they'd made it as far as the lake without waking a counselor with the slaps of their steps—and Jackson wore a bright white shirt that glowed like a spotlight. You looked them up and down, and shook your head with part pity, part amusement. "Amateurs," you said.

Nitin's smile back was bashfully apologetic. Jackson's shrug looked semi-defiant. You made them take off their flip-flops before we continued onto the dock, and Jackson his T-shirt too. He pulled it off slowly and smirked.

"A little overdressed now, aren't you?" he challenged. You slipped off your tank top and eyed his shorts—it was strip poker without the poker—and you both jumped in in your underwear.

Nitin and I stood there, fully clothed—except his feet—awkwardly watching-not-watching the two of you splash around, until I decided *fuck this* and dove in too. (Not a real dive—everyone knew there were rocks and shallow spots there, and diving head-first would be dangerous.) After a moment's hesitation, Nitin joined us with a perfect cannonball. I admit I enjoyed how much of it splashed in Jackson's face.

I was too shy to take off my top, but I felt pretty daring for dropping my skirt, which got soaked anyway when I pulled it back on after. I worried on our walk home how we'd explain if we got caught—our prefab excuse that I was saving you from sleepwalking wouldn't fly with our hair and my shirt dripping wet. But we didn't get caught. And part of me knew you would talk us out of trouble if it came to that.

Only Jackson stripped completely—and only once he was under-water, thank goodness—but the next day the whole camp knew we'd been skinny-dipping. (Hmm, I wonder who told them that?) I climbed out first to spare my virgin retinas getting burned with the sight of his bare ass. You stayed in, treading water, and the wind blew your soft laugh across the lake.

That was only about a week after we met them. Did you already love him then?

I still don't get it.

Tomorrow I start my junior year, and you . . . do not. It's weird and wrong in a million different ways.

This Back-to-School Eve feels lonelier than other years. Instead of wondering if this year I'll make any new friends, I'm missing the best one I lost. Instead of geeking out over school supplies and texting you possible outfits, I'm writing you a letter I'll never send and considering wearing first-day pajamas. Instead of hoping nobody notices the giant zit on my chin, I'll be walking down the halls wondering who knows about what happened.

I don't dread being called on at random this year. I dread being asked, "Hey, weren't you at that camp where someone got murdered?"

It's everywhere online. Most reporters aren't naming names, but so what when everyone else is. You and Jackson are famous. Infamous. Social media's worse than the news. Kids we barely spoke to keep posting all this shit—feeding rumors, leaking "evidence," sharing bullshit theories. Like they know anything about anything. Like they know anything about you.

All summer I loved how our names were always linked: Lainie and Kayla, Kayla and Lainie. No one mentioned me without you or you without me, except once they started mentioning Jackson. But even then. So people are talking about me now too. Reporters keep poking around. My parents' lawyer gave my only statement: No comment.

I send my calls straight to voicemail, then trash them, unplayed. There's only one person I would talk to, and you're not calling.

I deleted all my accounts, but it's still hard to look away. Of course I'm curious. Of course I'm constantly obsessing over who knows what and how, or thinks they do. Over when they'll announce the charges. Or whether they'll need me to testify—and if so, what I will or won't say.

Even now, I'm keeping your secrets. Every one that I can.

I saw your mom on TV today. A camera followed her from the parking lot into work. She ducked and shielded her face at first, then screamed at them to leave her alone. She looked wrecked. (The most disgusted I've ever seen you is when you said of your mom, "She just lets things happen to her. Lets them happen, then overreacts. She only fights back when it's too late. It's bad strategy, first of all. And second, it's pathetic. I will never be like her.")

"That poor woman," Adele said. "Kayla, honey, let's change the channel. You don't need to be watching this."

My parents have been treating me like an eight-year-old ever since they picked me up from camp. Under normal circumstances I would be annoyed, but it has been easier to just go along with it. They haven't really known what to do with me ever since I turned thirteen—their oldest patients are twelve, and my perfect brother stayed unnaturally good-natured through high school, so I'm the first moody teenager they've had to deal with.

("What do you think is the source of this unconscious hostility you're displaying?" Adele asked me, straight-faced, the first time I rolled my eyes in her presence. "What makes you think it's unconscious?" I shot back. It did not go over well.)

But this crisis, and my willingness to let them step in and take charge—to let my parents and the lawyer and Dr. Rita make the decisions for me, as long as they leave me alone—has been a break from all that. Adele and Peter are back in their comfort zone, and I . . . well, I'm in shock and mourning and depressed, if Dr. Rita's to be believed, and that saps a lot of energy. It's hard to care about being babied when you no longer care about anything at all.

Your mom was furious the first time I saw her too—the first day, moving into our cabin. We never talked about that (I guess now we never will), so I'm not sure if you noticed me the way I noticed you.

I don't remember the specifics. We must have introduced ourselves when we realized we were sharing a bunk, and probably our dads shook hands and chatted about traffic or something or other, but I can't conjure any of that now. The first time we said hi or whatever is lost to history, absorbed by the rafters and cabin walls covered in decades of initials, doodles, quoted lyrics, clever sayings. Girl graffiti.

What I remember most about the first time I saw you wasn't you, really, but your Teflon coating—that smooth, calm, impenetrable shield you built up around yourself like a force field, letting everything and everyone outside it bounce off. Your dad's distracted distance. Your mom's icy rage that shot out her pores like frozen daggers, piercing everything else around her. Everything except you.

The cabin was swarming with parents, siblings, and campers moving in. I was trying to make my bed without getting in anyone's way, when, a few feet behind me, your mom shouted at your dad, "Could you just fucking listen to me for once?" and everyone near us went quiet.

Your dad smiled vaguely, like her reaction was somehow amusing. Your mom threw up her hands and stormed outside, and the screen door slammed shut behind her. People stared while pretending not to. Your dad shrugged.

You went on folding your clothes into the dresser, as though none of it was happening—and if it was, it had nothing to do with you.

My parents widened their eyes at each other, ever so slightly. I could see they thought your mom was the problem. I could see they were flat-out wrong.

My parents might be clinical psychologists, but I'm a way better judge of most people than they are—at least, people over five feet tall. You used to joke I'm so hyper-observant because of all the TV I've watched, and we'd laugh, but I think there's something to that. All those true-crime shows and procedural dramas train the viewer to really notice other people's behaviors and tune into their thoughts. I'm pretty good at picking up on subtle cues that reveal people's feelings and motivations.

I didn't know the half of it with your parents, of course, but I could tell right away, weeks before you told me a single word about the divorce or your dad's affair, or how they'd shipped you off to Camp Cavanick so they could rip each other's lives—and yours—apart without having to factor you in at all, that your dad's checked-out obliviousness was an attack.

Not caring one way or another about a person who cares desperately about you is a perfect way to inflict a serious wound. It can push someone to extremes. Make them question their self-worth. Cause them to spiral with need.

I didn't sense that need in you yet. But I saw it in your mom, in how he'd pushed her to the edge and didn't care if she toppled over it.

She didn't have your Teflon talent.

I wonder if you chose me because at first you *wanted* to be seen.

Your Teflon took many forms over the summer—calm, charm, flirtation, evasion, fibs, stories, diversions, lies—but you never used it to protect yourself from me. Not until the end, until our big fight about you and Jackson, when you promised and apologized, hugged me, agreed, and shut me out.

It was the subtlest shift, but I felt it. Saw the light flick off in your eyes. You looked at me like I could be anyone.

That still hurts as much as the rest of this.

Here's another thing I don't get. All summer long, you wrapped us all around your little finger, tugged the strings in such a way that no one even minded having a puppet master. Everyone. Including me.

Except Jackson. He had you hook, line, and sinker—and every time he practiced catch and release, you swam back, begging to be hooked again.

Why did you ever let a guy like that take control of your heart?

You were so smart, Lainie. You were so *everything*. And you let him turn you into nothing. It's almost like you believed, deep down, you never deserved anything more.

You deserved so much better than this. I wish I could have made you see that, before it was all too late. I wish I still could.

I would give you the world if I had it.

Love,
Kayla

August 31, still (sort of)
(I guess technically September 1, but it never feels like the new day before dawn)
(I am not getting my beauty sleep. Here's hoping dark circles are in this year.)

Dear Lainie,

It's 2:53 a.m. and I have to get up for school in a few hours, but I can't sleep. I keep thinking about you and Jackson. Not the end of you and him, but the beginning. I'm still trying to understand how this whole horrible thing started, and why. Why you needed him like that when you had me.

I can figure out the when. It must have been a Saturday, because we were signing up for electives, and I guess it would have been the start of week four, since it most definitely was after the Fourth of July, but not right after, because that's the week you told people that outrageous story about the townie and the leftover fireworks and our late-night adventure at Burps and Brews, which never happened. But if it had, it would have been in the middle of week three. And Jackson wasn't part of our stories yet then.

I didn't notice the date because I didn't find meeting him significant. It was just a random day and he was just a random guy who you talked with while we waited for sign-ups.

He was behind us in line, but was Nitin with him? I don't remember. We might have met Nitin later. I think you asked about Jackson's shirt and he answered and we started talking, but I was only half paying attention to it all. I was distracted by bug bites and humidity and needing to pee. I probably noticed the basics: messy hair, hipster glasses, jawline mole (*beauty mark!*), southern accent. Kind of nerd hot, I guess, if you like scrawny guys in sci-fi T-shirts. Which apparently you did. Or at least, you liked this one. Maybe the cheekbones?

He asked what we were signing up for. "Tennis," you said, deadpan, though you hadn't touched a racket in your life.

He laughed and you were mock offended. "What, you don't believe me?" you said. He held up both hands, palms out, an apology. You backed down. "What are *you* signing up for?"

"Tennis," he said earnestly.

You both grinned. I scratched my ankle.

"Well, when it's our turn to volley, you'd best believe you're going down," you said.

"Oh yeah?"

"Yeah."

He stuck out his hand. This was a boy who liked a challenge—in that way, you were evenly matched. "Game on," he said. You shook on it.

It was our turn at the sign-up and of course all the pens were gone, but I'd brought one, having learned this might happen. I wrote my name and our cabin, put *improv* for my first choice and *silk-screening* second, dropped the slip in the box, and stepped aside for you to do the same. But you took my pen, wrote *TENNIS* in block letters, and turned it in, leaving the second line blank. So much for signing up together, like we'd discussed.

You handed my pen to Jackson, satisfaction mixed with a dare in your eyes, and walked away without bothering to see what he'd write. I stood there, torn between following after you and waiting to get my pen back. Jackson was staring at me, or through me. I shrugged and walked off.

I knew what he would write. I couldn't imagine anyone resisting you.

By the time I caught up, you'd forgotten him.

It was hot out. We went to the lake to swim.

Fin. (If only.)

You never think someone you know will get murdered like this, let alone that someone else you know will be the primary suspect. It's almost as unfathomable as killing someone yourself.

I mean, sure, I've had moments of panic when my parents were late to pick me up and my brain spun on every possible worst-case scenario, including picturing them bleeding to death from a robbery gone wrong. Or times when I made myself cry, thinking what it would be like if my brother got hit by a bus or caught in a school shooting. But I never really thought one of those things might happen. Imagining something awful in such morbid detail is supposed to make you safe from it actually coming true. I don't know how the science works, but it's like picturing disaster somehow prevents it.

Maybe my mistake was a failure of imagination. I completely failed to imagine on that day that Jackson would become significant. I didn't think to picture any of us ending up injured or heartbroken, let alone dead. And therefore, I failed to protect us.

When should I have seen it coming?

I watch a lot of true crime, but even that didn't prepare me for this. What I got from TV is: Women and girls are victims, and it is always, always the boyfriend.

But Jackson wasn't your boyfriend; he was someone else's. He'd told us early on about his girlfriend back home.

The Monday after your sign-up whim, you said only that tennis was "fine" but "too hot" before you changed the subject to the rumors about Chef Beverly, and I didn't know to notice. (There's no way a camp could hire a cook with a criminal record, though . . . is there? Even if it's just a small misdemeanor?)

On Tuesday you reported that Jackson was hilarious, and the two of you were planning a tennis revolt: new rules for the unathletic, which I listened to in detail, laughing along, though the nuance went over my head.

By Wednesday you were bubbling over about Terrible Tennis, the brilliant new game you two had invented, and how clever and amazing Jackson was. ("You'll love him. He's like me but a rich boy. Creative and super dark.") He and Nitin sat with us at campfire that night—Nitin and me toasting our marshmallows patiently, evenly, while you and Jackson stuck yours right in the fire, then dealt with the flaming mess.

I didn't love the new pairings suggested by our s'mores habits (you and I already seemed like a perfect set: one steady, the other ready to burn it all down), but I honestly wasn't threatened or worried. You told Jackson my weird skill of being able to hum while I whistle, and he kept trying to do it, and I kept trying to teach him, until we laughed so hard we nearly fell into the fire, and if anything, *you* were the one left out.

By the end of the week, you'd invited him and Nitin to sneak out with us. That night, walking back to our cabin under the tapestry of stars, the crickets chirping all around us (Me: "Did you know only male crickets chirp?" You: "No, Randy, I did not. Thank you for that whimsical knowledge bomb"), you hooked your arm through mine and asked, "What would I ever do without you?"

I laughed and said, "Well, you're stuck with me, so I guess we'll never find out."

How many things can one person be wrong about?

I know by the end you thought I hated Jackson, but I didn't. At the beginning, I almost liked him. I never found him as amazing as you did—or as he clearly found himself—but I liked that he was arty and strange. A little full of himself and not a great listener, but usually interesting enough and not horrible to have around. I wouldn't have chosen to invite him to hang with us, but I didn't object when you did. I thought you'd get bored with him eventually, the way you did with almost everyone else—especially once you realized he wasn't anywhere close to your league.

But the weirdest thing happened: He seemed to get bored with you instead.

I mean, not exactly. But while your interest in him intensified, his interest in you stayed right where it had started, and refused to budge. It's not that he wasn't into you. It's that Jackson's primary interest was always, and remained, himself. And I don't think you'd encountered that before—a person you couldn't charm into liking you exactly the amount you wanted them to.

I think maybe that's why you kissed him. To gain back the upper hand.

But after the kiss, you weren't just into Jackson. After the kiss, you were obsessed.

You hid it pretty well, how imbalanced things had become.

But I was the witness, the confidante. I was the one you could trust.

At night on the dock, you cried on my shoulder, or went manic with *fun* like to prove you didn't care—as if he was your audience even when we were alone together. I hated that. But I preferred it to the nights when he was with us, and your neediness multiplied like fruit flies on a rotten banana. Nights you begged me to come with you, only to sneak off with him alone, to do who knows what for who knew how long, while I waited in the dark to make sure you'd get home.

It hurt to watch you bend and twist, trying to prove you were enough for him. Trying to fit some idea of what he needed you to be. He was barely worthy of clinging to the bottom of your shoe, let alone making out with you. But he was what you wanted.

Each time he thoughtlessly stomped on your heart, I was there to pick up the pieces. I needed you, and if you needed me, I would be there every time. There was no on-again, off-again with you and me. Only Till Death Do Us Part.

But Lainie, as many times this summer as I wished Jackson gone, I never wished anyone dead.

Love,
Kayla

"It wasn't a secret. Everyone knew Jackson had a serious girlfriend back home. Lainie didn't seem to care about that. Neither did Jackson, for that matter."

"When you're at camp, all that matters is camp. I think what Lainie and Jackson had was real. They seemed really cute together, even though they fought a lot. It wasn't real fighting, though, just pushing each other's buttons. It was their thing. They were both competitive people. But they were so into each other. Anyone could see that."

"Lainie and Jackson's relationship ran super hot-and-cold. They'd be teasing each other one second, and breaking up again the next. Then ten minutes later you'd see them laughing and cuddling, or practically tearing each other's clothes off in public. You never knew what was serious or what was a huge joke with them. I think they both kind of fed off the drama, to be honest.

"This seems awful to say now, given what happened, but . . . that relationship couldn't have ended in anything but fireworks. They were explosive from the start."

"I guess I knew they hooked up, but I didn't know it was anything serious. Jackson flirted with anything that moved, and Lainie was always with Kayla. He was kind of slutty, if you ask me. I was surprised someone like Lainie would go for him. I thought she was way over his level.

"Sorry, I shouldn't have said that."

"I had no idea Jackson had someone else back home. I was shocked. But camp is this total bubble, you know? Like all that matters is who you are there, and nothing about back home feels relevant. You know? I don't know. It's hard to describe. It's not like I'm a different person at camp and with my camp friends. It's more like that I'm *more* of who I really am with them, because you come to camp without the baggage of people thinking they already have you all figured out. It's a clean slate. Nobody at camp knows anything about your past except what you tell them, but also, you know people *better* here. Your camp friends know you better than anyone else. Like, the real you. All that time you spend together is intense. You can live out a whole relationship in, like, a day."

"I have no idea what Lainie saw in him in the first place, but when they weren't fighting, they definitely made out a lot. I assumed it was just a summer thing, mostly physical. I never would have guessed either of them was invested enough for it to end so badly."

"I remember one meal, about a week before the end, when Jackson and Lainie had a huge fight over nothing. It started out kind of joking, a faux-fight over ketchup or something, but then he was saying X, and she was saying Y, and suddenly it got really serious, and we were all just like, whoa. It was super heated. Jackson definitely had a temper. They both did.

"Anyway. The fight was getting worse and she was all up in his face, just egging him on. And right when it seemed like he might actually, like, *hit* her, Kayla said something that sliced through the tension, and *bam*, it was over, just like that.

"Lainie joked back to Kayla and smiled at Jackson, and his cheeks stopped burning red. Soon they were kidding around like normal and I would have thought I misread it—that they weren't fighting at all, it was just some joke I wasn't in on—if it weren't for what happened later. If one of them hadn't turned up dead.

"I wish now I could remember more of what happened in that fight. I didn't think at the time it would be important. But Kayla was like that—she could defuse Lainie before she blew up. Which isn't how Lainie was normally, only how she got around Jackson. He really knew how to set her on fire."

September 4

Dear Lainie,

I made it through the first week of school, despite my unforgiving brain keeping me up until all hours, and my unforgiving alarm going off at 6:40, no matter what time I finally fell asleep. You used to rib me for being tired the mornings after we'd sneak out (I swear it's not human how much energy you always had), but you should see me now. Zombie city. It doesn't help that once I drag myself up and at 'em, the reward is another day of high school.

It feels different this year. Not the classes or the building or the pointlessness or the smell, but something. The vibe. I don't know if it's me, or what people think they know about me, but I'm finding it harder to be inconspicuous. Ironic that now that I *want* to slip through the days unseen, my classmates have suddenly noticed me. I guess once you cracked me out of my shell and rendered me uninvisible (uh, *visible*? Wow, good job, brain. Have I mentioned I need sleep?), it became impossible to go back. Or maybe it's literally you: Maybe they've seen the rumors in videos and comments online, and my proximity to the murder makes me seem different. I don't know.

This kid Jared, who I've never talked to, came up to me in the cafeteria today and said, "Hey, my cousin was at that camp with you." When I didn't respond, he added, "She said you were cool." It came out kind of accusatory, like I've been denying him and everyone else by holding back on my coolness all these years. I didn't know what to tell him. ("Uh . . . sorry?") I didn't ask who his cousin was. I just shrugged and walked away.

There's a new bulletin board outside the guidance office labeled "Wall of Shameless Brags." Ms. Heaton, the head counselor, put a little desk in front of it with sticky notes and pens (the pens disappeared in a day, so now there's only one of them, attached to the desk with string) and when there's something we're feeling proud of or glad about, we're supposed to write it on a Post-it and stick it on the wall, and feel all affirmed or whatever.

Ms. Heaton is way into it. The second morning, I walked by and saw she'd rearranged all the Post-its in the shape of a heart, and today they made a cresting wave. I think maybe Ms. Heaton should have been an elementary school art teacher instead of a guidance counselor. If she keeps this up, she won't have time to help anyone get into college.

The idea of it is cool, I guess. Positivity and self-esteem. It's true we're all socialized to sort of put ourselves down, or at least downplay our accomplishments. And there *shouldn't* be stigma around shouting about the stuff we're proud of, or being proud of who we are. But since no one signs their names to the Post-its and the brags are all anonymous, doesn't that kind of defeat the purpose? I feel like you would have a lot to say about that.

You'd think a school bulletin board with such an earnest mission would get abused pretty quickly, but people seem to be respecting it and keeping it positive so far. Either that or Ms. Heaton is monitoring it like a hawk.

Anyway, I made my first contribution to the brag board today. On my way back from chem lab, I wrote *I've held on to my best friend's secrets.* I stuck it in the wave, right at the crest, and wondered how long it could last.

Everyone thinks they know about you. They have no idea.

There are so many things I won't tell them.

Love,
Kayla

September 4
Channel 13 News

"This just in. Prosecutor Marsha Davis today filed charges of second-degree murder against sixteen-year-old Elaine Baxter, known as 'Lainie' or, more recently, as the alleged 'Summer Camp Slayer.' Maplewash County police arrested Baxter on August twenty-second in connection with the apparent murder of her summer-camp sweetheart, Jackson Winter, who was reported missing and found dead near Camp Cavanick grounds on August fourteenth. Although Baxter, at age sixteen, could still technically be considered a juvenile, the DA chose to file charges in adult court, due to the severity of the alleged crime and the defendant's history of low-level infractions, such as two previously undisclosed shoplifting charges.

"Baxter's court-appointed attorney, Michael Desir, said in a statement, 'Lainie is innocent of these terrible charges and welcomes the chance to clear her name in the upcoming trial. We have no further statement at this time.' At the arraignment, Baxter entered a plea of not guilty.

"The defendant remains in custody at the local juvenile detention facility where she has been held since her arrest. The judge set bail at two hundred thousand dollars, but the defendant's family has been unable to pay it.

"A spokesperson for the family of the deceased, Jackson Winter, asked for privacy and declined to offer comment at this time, other than to note they are still in mourning for a promising life cut tragically short."

September 5, 2:15 p.m.

Hey

It's Nitin

I don't know if we're allowed to talk or if you even want to hear from me but

I wanted to check if you're okay

Kayla?

hey

Hey

Sorry I didn't reach out sooner

this whole thing has been just

awful

I haven't known how to talk about it

words seem insufficient

I figured you're the one person who'd understand

You still there?

yeah

it's probably not a great idea for us to talk

sorry

Oh

okay

Take care of yourself then

                                        you too

yeah

September 6

Dear Lainie,

I knew this was coming, so it shouldn't be a shock, but it's still jarring to hear they've pressed charges. Your name out there in the media now. Charged as an adult. Branded a murderer.

It's all so official and real, but surreal, *unreal*, too. Four weeks ago, we were swearing to make the most of our last week at camp. To not even think about saying goodbye until the moment we had to—but even then, to be sad but not *too* sad, since the end of the summer wasn't the end of our friendship, just the beginning of its next chapter.

Now you're stuck in jail and Jackson is gone, and I'm forbidden by my parents' lawyer from contacting you.

I should do it anyway. I should get in the car and drive straight to your side. I should bang down the door and bribe all the guards, or whatever it takes to make them let me see you. I should stage a sit-in, a hunger strike, and insist they can't keep us apart.

I daydream about it. I imagine it's what you would do if our roles were reversed. But I'm scared.

I'm scared of what you might say if you saw me. I'm scared of what you might not.

I texted your number two weeks ago. It was already someone else's. I shouldn't have been surprised, but you can add that to the list of things I somehow didn't see coming.

Maybe it's safer that we're only talking like this, in my head, for now. But I hate that I can't reach you.

It's a ridiculous thing to focus on, but it makes me cringe, the fact that now everyone knows your real name. Maybe I'm stuck on it because the rest is too much to process, but I know you've always hated being called that. It's not a bad name; it's just not a *you* name. I remember how you described it: as the ultimate proof that your parents never understood you.

All summer, no matter who asked, you insisted that Lainie was your given name. Even Jackson and Nitin weren't let in on the truth, but to me you confessed it out of nowhere. You'd brought tea candles out to the dock that night, and we tried to shelter them with our limbs, but the wind kept gusting them out, so you kept relighting them. You were sparking the flame with your thumb when you said, "Can you believe my mother named me *Elaine*?" The wick caught and you glowed, then it blew out again.

Weirdly, of all the secrets you entrusted me with, that's the only one you made me swear to keep. And I did. But now everyone knows, and I hate that, possibly even more than you do.

You should get to be *you*. Though, granted, this whole thing isn't you—you're not a murderer. I know that. I hope you know I believe you, even if no one else does.

I didn't know about the shoplifting, though. Is that real or another stupid rumor?

I hate that I can't ask you. I hate that we can't talk about it. I hate that there's anything about you I don't know, and with each day that passes, there's more of it. We're both moving further and further from who we were over the summer. We're becoming who we are in the After.

DUN-DUH.

Sorry. That's the kind of thing that would have seemed deep and real if uttered out on the dock in the middle of the night, just you and me and the lake and the stars (and the occasional loon, plus crickets), but typed up it's melodramatic and ludicrous. MY BEST FRIEND HAS BEEN CHARGED WITH HER BOY-FRIEND'S MURDER AND I'M WRITING HER LETTERS I'LL NEVER SEND BECAUSE I MISS HER AND IT'S MY WAY OF MOURNING AND REMEMBERING OUR RELA-TIONSHIP. Okay, this whole situation is melodramatic to the extreme. Let's just acknowledge that.

Carry on, chap. (Your British accent was the worst. I miss that too.)

If you're wondering whether joking about this stuff is helping me freak out less, the answer is no, not really. It might be helping me hide it better, though. It seems important to at least try to hold myself together, though I don't know why or for who. But writing these letters does help in general. Dr. Rita was right about that. I feel less alone when I'm writing to you, and it helps me focus. Looking at the words gives me something present and real to concentrate on. It gives me a break from picturing you in a jail cell, or Jackson face-down in the lake. It lets me stop spinning on the morning after, and the things you said, and the things you didn't. It keeps my candle from blowing out in the wind.

Speaking of deep conversations on the dock, do you remember this one? It was after you got together with Jackson, but a night when only you and I were out. Maybe you guys weren't speaking, or maybe you were feeling nostalgic, so we snuck out just you and me. We were lying on our backs, looking at the sky, making up names of constellations.

You: "What do you want your legacy to be?"

Me: "My legacy?"

"Yeah. Like, once you're dead and gone, what do you want to be remembered for?"

"Besides discovering the Medium Dipper?"

"Yes, besides that."

I said the first thing that popped to mind. (You were right: My brain *is* random.) "I used to be able to burp the whole alphabet."

"Really? Wow."

I couldn't tell if you were teasing or being serious. No one has ever truly appreciated that talent, not even my brother. (I assume he was jealous.) "We can't all cure cancer," I said.

"I wouldn't ask it of you."

I paused before telling the truth. "Maybe I'd rather not be remembered."

I felt you roll your eyes at that one. "I think it's something we should be deliberate about," you said.

"Our legacies? Now?"

"If you don't decide and pursue it yourself, someone else will decide for you."

"That's fine. I'll be dead. I don't think I'll care," I said.

"*I* care."

"Okay, fine. What do you want your legacy to be?" I asked.

You shook your head. "I don't know. But I feel like I'm doing it wrong. Reaching for the wrong stuff. Failing at it."

We were quiet for a minute. I stared into the Milky Way. "I love who you are," I said. "I wish you did too. I wish you'd stop letting Jackson jerk you around. It's a game to him, and you can't win it. I hate when he makes you feel small."

I felt you stiffen, and held my breath. You let yours go and didn't fight me. "I know."

The silence felt warm and pliable around us. Maybe I should have pushed you harder then. I didn't.

I thought it was a turning point. I thought it was enough.

I pointed at the stars. "There's Antelope's Revenge."

"Mmm. Right next to the Maiden's Testicle."

"I love that one. Hanging just off the edge of the Chastity Belt," I said.

"I thought it was called Vulva's Crest."

"I think it's regional. Like 'pop' versus 'soda.'"

You sighed. "See, this is why I don't believe in science."

"Because dinosaurs claim the constellations were named through evolution?"

"Exactly," you said. I thanked my lucky stars that you'd found me.

You were right, though. You were reaching for the wrong things. Jackson had thrown you off track. And because of it, you lost control of your legacy. No matter how the trial turns out, you will always be remembered for this.

It changed my legacy too, by changing the course of our friendship and cutting it horribly short. Though it looks like I'll get my wish and be unremembered in the aftermath. No one ever remembers the role the sidekick played. I'm okay with that.

I only wanted to be central to and remembered by you.

That night, beneath the stars, I thought you would change course and follow a different constellation. Stop navigating by the light of Jackson and go back to shining bright on your own.

Not on your own—with me beside you. Two stars in Vulva's Crest. (Ew. Never mind, let's join the Medium Dipper.)

I want to believe this could still end differently.

Love,
Kayla

P.S. I heard from Nitin yesterday. Maybe you're right, maybe he did have a thing for me. I don't think so, though. I think he was being kind, or needed someone to talk to and flip out with.

Either way, I shot him down. I'm not supposed to talk to anyone but Dr. Rita or my parents about you, not without the lawyer present. Not that I'd want to anyway. I only want to talk to you.

I'm worried I'll get called to testify. I don't know what that would be like. Even with Dr. Rita, I've told the truth but not the whole truth.

I don't like to think about some of it. I'd rather ignore the parts that don't add up.

There are pieces of this story I don't want to be true, and truths I don't think I'll ever understand. I don't want to talk about those. It makes my throat close up and my eyes sting just thinking about it. And I've never been a good liar. Not compared to you.

September 10
Now Today

FROM THE OUTSIDE, ELAINE BAXTER SEEMS LIKE THE
kind of girl anyone might kill to be, or be with: Friends say she's more
than just beautiful. She's also smart, adventurous, entertaining, and
fun.

But the charismatic sixteen-year-old is not only vivacious; she is
also, by many reports, troubled. Some of her peers describe her as
a skilled storyteller, while others paint her as having a loose relationship with the truth. Prosecutors in the Jackson Winter murder
case have suggested there's a simpler word to describe her: *liar.* They
say the statement Baxter gave police the morning Winter's body was
found—a statement she later retracted when it became clear how
many holes and errors it contained—was only one of many deceptions the suspect attempted to spin over the course of that fateful
summer. They say the "disturbing pattern" of false and misleading
stories Baxter is alleged to have told is "just the tip of the mountain of
evidence" they will share with the jury at trial, as they work to prove
beyond the shadow of a doubt that Baxter's claims of what really happened between her and Jackson Winter the night of August thirteenth
are not to be believed.

Baxter's lawyer describes the police's early focus on his client as
the primary suspect in the investigation as a "witch hunt" and suggested Baxter should not only be found innocent, she should be
considered, "if anything, the second tragic teenage victim in the case."

But as more conflicting stories emerge from fellow campers and former classmates, many who thought they knew her say they're left asking: Who *is* Elaine Baxter, and could she really be capable of murder?

We'll soon find out. Jury selection for Baxter's trial is set to begin October 22. A spokesperson for the family of the slain teenager, Jackson Winter, says they remain devastated over the loss of their beloved brother, nephew, grandchild, and son, and hope that at last the full truth about the circumstances surrounding his death will emerge in court.

Camper and Counselor Interviews, Statements, and Posts
August 14–November 24

"Lainie loved a good story, especially if she was the one telling it. I don't think she cared so much if the story was actually true."

"I knew Lainie pretty well. I mean, she was in my cabin the whole time. I had the top bunk on the bed next to hers and Kayla's. But all the stuff in the news and the things people are saying, it doesn't match up with the Lainie I thought I knew. Like, some of the stuff she told us made it seem like she came from a lot of money, and now it turns out the opposite is true. And I'm just like, *why*? About all of it. But about that stuff, the little stuff, too. It feels like we might never know the whole truth about her."

"Lainie was always telling wild stories. I loved to hear her talk. She could be telling you what she had for breakfast and she'd make it seem like the most exciting thing around, like eating oatmeal was an adventure you wished you could go on too. I don't think that makes her a liar. It made her interesting."

"I've never met anyone so charismatic. She was just *likable*, and the stories she told were part of that, even if some were exaggerated. Isn't that what they say about all psychopaths, though? That they're always charming? I think I heard that on a podcast once."

"I'm not surprised she turned out to be a liar and a murderer. Everyone thought she was so great, but she was too good to be true, you know?

"I don't say that just because of me and Jackson. Even if he hadn't had a thing with Lainie, I wouldn't have kissed him again. *I'm* not a boyfriend thief. We were caught up in a moment, that's all. It never happened again."

"Ugh, you shouldn't listen to a word Emma says about Lainie. She thinks hooking up with Jackson *once* made her an expert on them both. Like, hello, sucking face with a notorious fuckboy doesn't show you the depths of his soul, let alone make you an authority on the other girl he's been cheating on his girlfriend with.

"Lainie might have spun a few tall tales, but Emma was downright delusional. She still won't let it go."

"This whole thing feels like a story she might tell, one that keeps everyone gasping and guessing until the end. She was always in control of every twist and turn, and good at manipulating audiences too. People ate it right up, whatever she'd tell them, no matter how outrageous the story got. When she told it, you'd be all wrapped up in listening, and maybe after you'd have a moment of *Wait, could that really be true*? But she made you want to believe her, every word of it. And often it was like, well, it must be true, because who would invent something like that?"

September 11

Dear Lainie,

I remember the first time I watched you lie. Or rather, the first time I saw it and *knew* you were lying. The first time I was an accomplice, not a witness.

Before that, there were other times. Times when I wasn't certain, just confused—when it seemed like your stories didn't quite match up or that if they contained truth, you were probably stretching it. Like that time you told the story about your cat.

The cat story was harmless. (They all seemed harmless to me, all summer, until the last one.) People were hanging out in the mess hall after lunch, talking about ways adults can be clueless. Obvious double entendres going over a sex ed teacher's head; parents trying to be hip about music; a chaperone who believes the bottle being passed around a bus contains only water. That kind of thing. It was the first week, and everyone was trying to show off how edgy and cool they could be. But you didn't care about cred.

You told us about the time your cat was off roaming the neighborhood, and another black cat came in through the cat door and made himself at home in your house. Your parents fed him and petted him and called him by your cat's name, and nobody believed you that "This isn't Stormy!" Until Stormy came back home hours later.

Your parents looked back and forth between the stray cat on the couch and *your* cat entering the living room, hissing and raising his fur at the intruder. Your mom's jaw dropped and your dad blinked rapidly, like that might clear his double vision. The stray cat stretched and yawned, lifted his leg, peed on the sofa, then bolted out the door. Your dad blinked one more time and went back to his iPad. Your mom cleaned up the mess. Neither of them spoke of it again.

I laughed with everyone else, but later, when it was just us, asked, "I thought you said your parents wouldn't let you have a pet."

"Oh, they won't," you said cheerfully. "My mom's allergic to everything, or claims she is. I think she just doesn't like animals or messes, but whatever. That's my friend's story about the cats. It really happened. Everything except the peeing part."

"But you told it like it's yours," I said, feeling slow.

"Yeah. It's a better story that way," you said. And of course you were right.

The first time I was in on it happened a few days later, in week two. You didn't warn me in advance, but I think it was spur-of-the-moment. Most of your lies weren't premeditated.

The night before, we'd snuck out for the fourth or fifth time. Our escapes happened regularly, but not every night, and not on a schedule I could predict. It was all according to your whims. I didn't mind. The uncertainty was part of the excitement.

That night I expected to follow you down the hill, onto the dock, where we'd always gone before. I already thought of the dock as Our Place, even though a hundred people or more used it in daytime. But you turned left out our cabin door and went up the path toward the road. I hustled after you.

"Where are we going?" I whispered once we'd gotten a safe distance away. The moon was full, low, and bright. The brightness felt dangerous, like a spotlight was on us.

You weren't worried about hiding. You walked down the center of the empty dirt road and opened your arms to the galaxy. You twirled before acknowledging my question. "To town," you said.

"How?" Town was a few miles away, and neither of us was dressed for civilization. We'd look like fugitives in our pajamas, even if it weren't clearly past our bedtime. (It was past everyone in Jasper-town's bedtime. Early bedtime's the whole point of rural life.)

You shrugged. "We'll hitchhike. Find a bar where we can dance with the locals."

I stared at you. "Are you serious?"

You grinned and held out your hand. "If I am, will you go with me?"

I took the offered hand. You spun me like the road was our dance hall. "It's one a.m. I highly doubt anything is open around here at this hour," I said.

You released me and kept walking. "Maybe not. But I was kid-ding. I don't need townies. I've got you."

"Thanks?"

"It's a compliment," you confirmed. "I choose your company above all others. You're welcome, dah-ling." I glowed. You tipped your head at me. "I just wanted to go for a stroll. I get restless stuck in one place. Is that cool?"

"It's cool."

We walked to the end of the road and back, sometimes talking, sometimes not, and went back to the cabin and slept. That was it.

The next morning, Maddie interrogated us at breakfast. "I saw you guys sneak back in last night. Where'd you go?"

I made my eyes round with innocence, but you didn't try to deny it. Instead, straight-faced, you said, "We hitchhiked into town."

Maddie's face was pure shock. A few other people turned to listen. You hadn't kept your voice down. "Are you serious?" she asked.

You lifted your eyebrows with mild surprise. "Of course," you said.

Maddie looked to me for confirmation. I shrugged. I was curious to hear where you might take this.

"You went along with that?" Maddie pushed.

You answered for me. "Actually, it was Kayla's idea."

I shoved a forkful of egg in my mouth to stop my face from reacting.

"Wow," Maddie said. She looked at me with new respect.

Another camper leaned across the table. (Is it possible that was Emma? She wasn't relevant yet, so there's no reason for me to have noticed her. This was long before we met Jackson. But when I replay this memory, I picture her strongly—already lurking around, just waiting for you to acknowledge her, or whatever the fuck her deal was.)

"Weren't you scared? Especially out so late?" Emma or Not-Emma asked. (Do I only remember her there and at other weird moments because of the shit that came later? I don't know. I'm clearly biased, so perhaps my memory can't be trusted. But I'd bet you anything it's right.)

"Yeah. What if you got picked up by an ax murderer?" Maddie said.

You shook your head. "I had Kayla there to protect me. The odds of *two* ax murderers on one country road have got to be very slim."

Everyone laughed and you told them about the night we'd had. The bar's old-fashioned jukebox with no songs from after 1992. The sawdust on the floor. The college guys we ignored to dance only with each other. The pixieish bartender with a unicorn tattoo who gave us a ride at the end of her shift. We told her we lived on Landon Lane, so she dropped us off there and we walked the rest of the way.

I was sure they would know it was bullshit, but they ate it up, staring at us with awe.

"Did they serve you?" someone asked.

"Just a Sprite," you said. "And Kayla had a virgin daiquiri." You winked, but no one else caught it.

It's funny: As you told that story, I almost believed it. I started feeling kind of jealous of this adventure you'd had without me. But that wink was a reminder we were in on this together.

"I still wish I'd kept the paper umbrella," I said with a sigh. I've always been a terrible liar, but it came out smooth. People believed my embellishment. I felt a thrill of power.

I get why you told those stories. It was fun. You enjoyed the rush. You liked being the center of attention, and pulling one over on everyone else. The power trip of making people laugh—making them believe you—was addictive. You were interested in seeing how much you could get away with, how far you could push the truth. It was a way of protecting yourself too. A version of the Teflon.

Your stories were a shield. They kept anyone else from knowing you in ways you didn't want them to.

I didn't mind. I played along. And I loved being the only one who knew the truth. It made our nighttime escapes all the more *ours*. It made the secrets you confided seem all the more intimate.

Once, when I reacted with "I can't believe you told them that. I can't believe they believed it," I remember what you said.

"Look. They *want* to believe I'm outrageous. They want life to be as interesting as I make it sound. They don't want a girl like me to be just like everyone else. They want excitement. So I let them have it. I'm giving the people what they want! And I'm less bored this way. Everyone's happier in the end."

That seemed true. The one or two times your embellishments got called out, you didn't dig in or get embarrassed. You gave the kind of smile that invited others in on the joke, and said, "But it makes a better story that way, doesn't it?" And it only made people like you more.

I wasn't there when you lied to the cops the morning after Jackson died, but I know why you did that too. You were scared. No one really knew what had happened yet—only that Jackson was dead and everyone was freaking out and the police had questions, especially for those who knew him best. You. Me. Nitin. His counselors. The other guys in his cabin. Anyone who might be able to shed light on what appeared to be a tragic accident.

There was a rumor he'd dived off the dock into a rock, though there were "No Diving" signs all over and everyone knew it was shallow in places. Jackson was a decent swimmer, but not with a head wound.

It was all so shocking and impossible to comprehend, and you especially were in a daze. Only alone with me did you let yourself get hysterical. I couldn't do anything to ground you. You just weren't thinking straight.

It was the first time I'd seen you truly panic.

No one had said the word *murder* yet. People weren't thinking of his death as suspicious. Not even the police. So it makes perfect sense to me: Of course you lied. The third rule of crime is Don't Get Caught, and we'd been covering our tracks expertly all summer. We had been in that mode for eight weeks by that point. It wasn't easy to just switch out of it.

You probably told those lies on autopilot, out of habit and fear of getting caught. Not caught for killing him—caught sneaking out of our cabin after lights-out. There wasn't any use confessing that and stirring up *more* trouble.

You told the cops you'd kissed him goodnight outside our cabin before curfew. And you had. (The best lies are built on truth, even if those aren't the most entertaining ones.) You just didn't mention kissing him again—and more—when you met up again later as planned.

That omission, when they discovered it, turned the cops' full suspicions on you. They had a lot more questions after that, and a lot more trouble believing you.

When they asked around, they learned you'd been stretching the truth all summer. Things really snowballed from there.

It was shit luck. Telling stories isn't a crime—or it shouldn't be. And even if you're a liar, that doesn't make you a murderer. Though from the way some people are talking, it's practically hard, admissible evidence. (I can see you rolling your eyes and saying, "Of course they are." The perfect dismissal.)

For some reason that morning I asked you, "Was he alive the last time you saw him?" You looked stunned and said, "Are you kidding? Yes." I believed you.

I still do.

Love,
Kayla

Camper and Counselor Interviews, Statements, and Posts
August 14–November 24

"I don't think it could have happened the way everyone says it happened. Like, why would you *kill* someone over something like that? I think it must have been an accident or, like, bears or something, I don't know."

"My first week at camp I was totally scared to walk back to the cabin or to the bathrooms alone after dark. I always made someone go with me. People told all these stories at campfire one night, and it freaked me out.

"There's a counselor who drowned in the lake a long time ago, and his ghost still haunts the boathouse. When he cries, it sounds like the loons at night. You can hear them across the lake. Not to mention ax murderers.

"I heard a noise the first week, and I really thought there might be someone or something hiding in the woods, waiting to kill us. I never thought to be scared of other campers, though.

"I don't think my parents will send me back next year. This kind of ruined camp for a lot of us, you know?"

"How come nobody's talking about Nitin? Where was he that night? He and Jackson seemed tight for the first part of camp, but I never saw them together toward the end. If they had some kind of falling-out, that might be relevant. I don't know. Nitin always seemed nice, but that's suspicious too. Like, he almost was *too* nice for Jackson. I don't know what they had in common, besides being in the same cabin.

"It's always the quiet ones you have to look out for."

"The night we hooked up, Jackson told me about Lainie's temper. We didn't talk about her much because we were . . . you know . . . but that's one thing he said. 'That girl has a major temper,' or something like that.

"He wasn't afraid of her or anything but, like, maybe he should have been. All these people talking about 'maybe it was an accident' or 'maybe it was Nitin' or maybe it was *me*, even, need to face the facts. She had a temper. She had a temper and she killed him. End of story.

"I can't believe I hooked up with him a few weeks ago and now he's *dead*."

"I thought their relationship seemed really passionate. To be honest, I was kind of jealous. I wanted to have a summer romance that interesting and dramatic.

"Now I don't know what to think."

September 13

Dear Lainie,

I'm supposed to be writing a persuasive essay, due tomorrow, on whether cell phones should be allowed in school, but I'll most definitely be asking for an extension and telling Mr. Rabbani it's been hard for me to focus on anything but you.

So far my teachers have been very understanding about the "extenuating circumstances" affecting my academic performance. I've been doing less work, yet making better grades, than at any other point in my high school career. So, thanks for that, I guess?

I would much rather still be a plain old, regular slacker and have my best friend back. No lie.

Ugh.

Here's something you told us that still makes me laugh, even if it's fake: the kid you went to school with whose name is Groovy Nipples.

We were out on the dock—a warm night. I remember you had your feet in the water and it splashed if you kicked when Jackson tickled you now and then. Nitin and I were commiserating about our teachers' faces lighting up when they realized we were related to our exceptional older siblings, and that sinking feeling we'd get, knowing the bar had been raised too high and we were guaranteed to fall—splat!—on our asses right below it.

You lifted your head off Jackson's shoulder. "It could be worse," you said. "Your parents could have named you Groovy Nipples."

No one pointed out the non sequitur. "Groovy Nipples is not a name," I said, looking away from Jackson's fingers sliding up your back, under the tank top, as though Nitin and I weren't right there, less than three feet away.

"It absolutely is," you said, "unfortunately for Groovy Nipples Eaton." You told us about the girl at your school whose parents were total hippies and probably high off the birth meds and who knows what else when they named her.

"Is Nipples, like, a middle name? And Groovy is her first name?" Nitin asked, squinting like that would bring the answers into focus.

"No, it's one name, like Mary Kate or Wilma Sue."

"Okay, no one is named Wilma Sue," I said. You shrugged.

Jackson nuzzled your neck. Nitin shot me a quick eye-roll and I liked him more than ever, but that didn't mean I wanted to be handed off on him. If we were grouping off in twos, that wasn't the correct pairing. Everyone except me seemed to have missed or forgotten that. (Though Nitin might have preferred you or Jackson at that point; who knows.)

"Does she have siblings?" I asked, to pull you back to us.

"An older brother. Paul."

I shook my head. "Is that true?"

You pulled your feet from the water and swiveled to face me. Jackson turned too. He looked bored now that he wasn't groping you. "Do you want it to be?" you asked.

"That's not an answer," I said.

You wiggled your toes. "Truth is stranger than fiction, Randy."

Jackson poked you in the side and you dodged his fingers and giggled, gasping for breath when he went for the full tickle.

It was fake. You weren't ticklish. I knew *that* was true. We'd had a whole conversation about "mind over matter" and your conviction that ticklishness is all in one's head . . . though I'm still hopelessly ticklish and haven't been able to train myself out of it, even with your best attempts at coaching me. I'm weaker-willed than you, I guess.

I'd tested you, though, and you were a woman of steel through all my little pokes and jabs and scuttles and soft touches. Never breaking, no matter where I ran my fingers. You were faking it for him, to stroke his ego or keep his attention, and that was annoying to watch, like all PDA—but it also made me a bit smug. He thought he could control you, but I knew you were the one manipulating him.

"Why do you call her that?" Jackson asked when the tickles had stopped and you'd tucked yourself against him.

"What?" you said.

"Randy."

You sneak-attacked with a nudge of tickles in his side. His giggle was high-pitched. That form of excuse to touch each other was getting old, fast. "Why do you think?" you teased.

Jackson grinned. "Because she's so randy? Like, horny all the time?"

I wanted to vomit. You rolled your eyes. "Yes, it's a comment on the perpetual wetness of Kayla's vagina," you said, your voice dry. I would have been okay, I think, if you'd stopped there, but you went on. "Randy is uncommonly lascivious," you added. "She whacks off so hard our whole bunk bed shakes. And you should hear the moaning. It lasts all through the night." Nitin shifted uncomfortably and I shot daggers that bounced right off you as you and Jackson laughed.

Guys like Jackson love it when a girl talks about sex, no matter what she's saying. It fogs their brains and stimulates their salivary glands and distracts them from anything else that's happening. You knew that and played it to your full advantage. You used me in that moment to draw Jackson to you.

I hated it. I had to look up the word *lascivious* later (I'm certain Jackson didn't know it either), but even without a dictionary on hand, the gist—and your intentions—were clear. It took my breath away. I'd never been the butt of your jokes before. You were thoughtless with plenty of people, but you'd never been thoughtless toward me. And for what? To impress Jackson for five seconds? Was that worth humiliating your best friend?

My cheeks burned in the dark and I considered getting up and leaving, but then you pulled away from Jackson. You reached for my hand and squeezed it. "Sorry to tell them your secret," you said. "You know it's that I live my life in truth."

Nitin snorted. Jackson looked confused. "It's okay," I said. I squeezed back. "People were bound to find out eventually. All that gushing. The randy waterfalls. The way I talk about sex twenty-four seven."

You shook your head solemnly. "You need help, Randy. But I still love you."

"I love you too. You and your groovy, groovy nipples."

Your laughter then was real.

I looked for Groovy Nipples Eaton online today, wondering if she could possibly exist. I couldn't find her through Google or on social media, but if I were named Groovy Nipples, I would use a nickname or go into hiding. I did find a real person named Gruvi Nipples Paulekas, who was born in 1967 and had a little brother named Freakus (or Phreekus), if the internet is to be believed. Maybe you'd heard about her and removed the degrees of separation. Not a complete lie, exactly.

Like you said: Truth is stranger than fiction.

At any rate, with that hand squeeze, you squashed my irritation. It was you and me versus them and everyone else again. Maybe you'd never meant to humiliate me, only to keep the others out of what was ours. It was none of Jackson's or Nitin's business why you called me Randy. You'd offered up a lie to protect our secret.

You were under Jackson's spell, but not completely—not yet. It wasn't too late then to pull you back to me.

Sometimes I think maybe it's still not too late. That if I can find the right words to get through to you, we will find our way back to how things were before.

But what if we can't?

Fuck Jackson for all that came after.

Love,
Kayla

Camper and Counselor Interviews, Statements, and Posts
August 14–November 24

"I never noticed Jackson before he started hanging with Lainie and Kayla. Then it was like, *Oh yeah, there's that guy who has a thing with Lainie.* I assumed he must be cool for her to be into him, but I don't know. She could have gone out with anyone."

"I don't think their relationship was actually all that imbalanced. You never know what's really going on in someone's head, right? Or what a couple is like when they're alone together. I've known lots of couples who break up and get back together and break up and get back together. We're in high school. It's like that. It didn't seem weird or outrageous to me, and I don't remember anyone saying that stuff at the time. I think people just look at it differently now because he's dead. Once something like this happens, you only remember the extremes."

"I never actually spoke to Jackson, but I hate him over what he did to Emma. Not the hookup, but the way he treated her after. He told the guys in his cabin, 'She's hot but she kisses like a fish.' Which, first of all, what does that even mean? And second, way to be a total asshole. His friend Nitin stepped up and said, 'Not cool, man,' which stopped the laughter, and a few other guys backed Nitin up. Jackson said he was only kidding and Emma is great, and switched to insulting Nitin.

"It got back to her and of course she was completely humiliated.

She said it was fine, but it wasn't. I saw and heard her crying. I hated that guy. I'm not sorry.

"I'm pretty sure he was the source of those stupid rumors about Chef Beverly too."

"I don't want to speak ill of the dead or whatever, but what you see of Jackson on the news isn't the whole story. Nobody's perfect and he was just another teenage guy—he could be a real jerk sometimes, and he was pretty smug and self-centered. Or maybe that was all posturing because he was deep-down insecure, I don't know. I shouldn't psychoanalyze him. But the way he treated Lainie sometimes, I don't know why she put up with it. I guess she didn't, in the end. I'm not saying he deserved to *die*, that's ridiculous. But he wasn't some perfect saint like you'd think from the eulogies. He wasn't even especially nice. Or, he was fine, but he was kind of a jerk to his friends—always sarcastic, and making 'jokes' that were really just insults—and shouldn't your friends be the people you're nicest to? I don't know. I guess he wasn't my type of person. I avoided him as much as possible, which was hard since we were in the same cabin."

"My mom says some women like to be treated badly because they can't see their own self-worth. That sounds like victim-blaming, but I think maybe with Lainie it was true. She seemed so confident and untouchable with everyone else, but Jackson was her weak spot. Her Achilles heel. It was like the worse he acted, the more she wanted him. Maybe she put up with his shit because on some level she thought she deserved it. Until the end. Then she just snapped."

"This one time I saw Lainie throw a soda in Jackson's face. Just sloshed it right at him. They were fighting about something and he started mimicking her voice, like '*mih mih mih*,' all high-pitched and stupid, and the next second he was sitting there, dripping wet. Soda and ice.

"Everyone froze, super tense, and Kayla looked back and forth between them like, *Oh shit, here we go*. Then Jackson cracked up out of nowhere and Lainie did too. Someone clapped and Jackson stood up and took a bow, but . . . it could have gone very differently. They both had tempers, and honestly, they were kind of attention whores. If she hadn't killed him, I could just as easily imagine the opposite: that he'd be the one to kill her. And if she did really do it, I wouldn't be surprised to learn it was self-defense. There was a lot more to both of them than meets the eye."

September 24

Dear Lainie,

The idea of you killing Jackson became a thing pretty early on. I think it started when he told us about his allergies. "So if I wanted to kill you, I should just eat a PB&J and slip you some tongue?" you joked one day at lunch.

"The kiss of death. At least I'd die happy," he said. You two were having a good day. On again, for the moment.

"Or you could wear a cat-fur coat and rub up against him," I said. You blinked at me like you'd forgotten I was there.

"Nah, then I'd just get itchy-eyed and snot-nosed. Maybe break out in a rash," he explained.

"Sexy," you said.

"That's my middle name."

"Weird. I wonder if we're related," I said. It worked. You laughed.

Sometimes I wonder if you and Jackson would have kept getting back together if I'd refused to play the third wheel—the kind that smooths out the ride and keeps the tricycle steady. I was the reliable anchor that allowed you to spin faster, faster, without worrying whether you might topple over and crash.

Maybe I should have set you loose. Been my own unicycle or whatever. But that wasn't the way of us. And in truth, I liked feeling needed. I liked being the one you depended on, no matter what. The one you always returned to.

I played the part that was asked of me, from the start.

"So tell us about this girlfriend. *Meghan*," I said the first night we hung at campfire with him and Nitin.

You shot me a look, but it was all for show. You had asked me to bring her up. You wanted to know more about her, but you didn't want to be the one to ask.

"Randy! That's Jackson's private business," you said. You blew out your flaming marshmallow and pulled off its charred-to-carbon skin.

"Sorry," I offered.

"No, that's okay. I don't mind talking about her," he said.

I looked to you for direction. You accepted the package of graham crackers from Nitin and focused on crafting your s'more. I took that as a sign to continue.

"How long have you guys been together?" I asked.

"Since the end of freshman year," he said. "I'd had an enormous crush on her for months, but she barely noticed I existed. I did all this stuff to try to get her attention, but none of it ever worked. She just thought I was some nerdy doofus."

"I mean, she's not exactly wrong on that," you said.

Jackson smirked. "Says the girl who had a whole Tumblr devoted to the *Supernatural* fandom."

(Was that true? If you did, I haven't been able to find it.) You shrugged and sucked marshmallow goo off your fingers. Jackson watched.

"So what happened? What changed her mind?" Nitin asked. He looked as invested in the story as you looked indifferent to it.

"About a month before the end of school, we got paired up for a World History project. We had to spend all this time together working on our presentation, and like halfway through the week she kind of narrowed her eyes at me and said, 'You know, you're a lot smarter than you usually act. If you were more like this on a regular basis, I might even give you a chance.'"

"Wow," Nitin said. (Prediction: It will take Nitin *years* to make a move on whoever he falls for—like, the person will have given up on their crush and assumed he's not interested, because he'll be so polite and shy and also miss all that person's signals. But once they finally get together, it will be true love forever and he'll be the king of grand romantic gestures for the rest of their natural lives. And possibly all of eternity as a ghost. Doesn't he seem like the type?)

"We've been together ever since," Jackson said. "She's amazing."

Your face displayed exactly zero reaction, but I noticed a slight twitch in your hand, like the declaration made your fingers jumpy. You took a bite of s'more. The marshmallow oozed out the sides.

"Sounds serious," I said, slowly rotating my stick to keep its marshmallow toasting evenly. Nitin caught my eye and smiled.

"Yeah." Jackson stared into the flames, looking contemplative. He didn't seem to notice his marshmallow was on fire. "In a way, this summer feels like . . . I dunno. Like my last chance at freedom or something. Not that Meghan isn't fun. But we got serious really fast. This is the longest we've been apart, by far. It's weird. Weird but good." The remains of his marshmallow slid off and hit the ground.

If you weren't into him, we'd have talked smack later—or possibly then—about him acting like his clearly awesome girlfriend was the rain on his parade. But you *were* into him. Your eyes shone triumphant.

"What's she doing this summer?" Nitin asked.

Jackson kicked some dirt over his fallen marshmallow. Someone probably stepped on it later and made their sandals a sticky mess. "She's in Italy. Her cousins have a place on the Amalfi Coast. So she's not sitting around missing me, either."

"Wow," Nitin repeated.

You didn't look impressed. "Oh, Italy. Everyone's so into it, but France is a million times better. Have you been to Paris?" you asked. We all shook our heads. "Best place in the world," you declared.

I knew for a fact you had never left the country—you'd barely left the state—but I didn't let on. This show was not for me.

"I might go there for college," you continued. "Whenever I'm in France, it just feels like the place where I belong."

"You speak French?" Nitin asked. He was such a gullible sweetheart.

"*Mais oui*," you replied.

"*Oh là là*," I said.

Nitin smiled, but Jackson seemed bored now that we weren't talking about him. He stood and wiped his hands on his shorts. "My butt cheeks are falling asleep on this log. You wanna walk?" he asked, looking at you.

You glanced at me to see if I minded. I kept my face as neutral as yours had been before. So you did what you wanted.

"Sure." You reached out a hand to let him pull you up beside him. Nitin and I watched as you disappeared together into the dark.

Jackson had wanted a carefree summer, and at first you were a huge part of that. At first you *were* his freedom. But soon you became a threat to it. He couldn't be free if you and he were attached.

So you pretended you weren't. You went along with it being a fling. But it wasn't. He knew that.

It wasn't just a fling for him, either. And he couldn't handle that at all. It contradicted everything he'd been trying to prove.

I think Jackson Back Home was a devoted boyfriend who worked hard to live up to Meghan's standards, because being a good boyfriend didn't come naturally to him. She was way above his level, and he knew it, so he constantly hustled to prove himself worthy. It was exhausting. He was scared to fail and lose her, but he was also tired. He wanted a summer of just being a selfish prick. Which meant *not* becoming a good boyfriend to you.

He wanted you to be hot and fun and accommodating and easy, and keep your needs and emotions to yourself. Those were the terms. And for some reason, you accepted them. You bottled yourself up in front of him, and only let things spill over in jokes, or with me.

I hated the mess he made of you. Hated how precisely he slid the knife up under your ribs to slice you open with a gesture, a comment. Hated that you handed him the weapon to do so in the first place. You kept pretending you were down with whatever, that it was no big deal and just a game to you too—which meant you couldn't ever ask him to stop.

Even when you bickered or pouted or sort of fought back, you were playing the part he wanted you to play. The part of the girl who could have had anyone, but lost her shit over him.

I think Jackson loved the drama. That's why he was into you in waves, his attention flooding in and out like high tide and low. Running his hands all over you, then remembering he had a girlfriend and acting like that was *your* fault, when in truth what he wanted was for you to beg and assure him she didn't matter.

He wanted you to pull him back, be irresistible, so his giving in and cheating again could be blamed on you. After all, you knew he was taken. It wasn't his fault you kept throwing yourself at him like that, swearing you understood it could never be something real. Listening to him go on and on about how much he loved her, while he was touching you. Reassuring him he was a good person because he felt tortured by his betrayal. Agreeing that what you had together existed in a separate universe from him and her. It wasn't cheating—it was fate, and it would only last the summer.

UGH.

You played it cool, but I watched it eat away at you. It was my job to do triage while you spun and obsessed, and that ate away at me too. But your drama wasn't about me. I was just the best friend.

When I finally convinced you to scrape up your dignity and stop letting him play this game, he turned around and made out with Emma.

Poor Emma. You'd barely even noticed her worshipping at our feet all summer, wishing she could be you. But Jackson noticed. It made her easy prey when he needed a willing target to be part of his sleazy revenge.

Jackson needed a new groping post. She leaped to volunteer.

You didn't blame her for that—you're not a hypocrite. And besides, she was only thirteen. You laid your wrath on Jackson, where it belonged.

It's the one time the joke about killing him didn't seem like only a joke.

You grumbled under your breath about wanting to slice him to pieces, and I suggested ways to make it as painful and humiliating as possible. We killed him a thousand times in our minds in gruesome, graphic detail, until you could look at him across the mess hall with Emma clinging to his side and laugh, genuinely laugh.

His deaths were a rebirth. They brought you back to *you*.

I thought you'd gotten over it—the worst of it, anyway. You stopped mentioning his name every eight seconds. You got swept up in your usual schemes. Your mood improved to a high that was almost manic. I caught you *humming*.

I should have known. But I was happy you were happy, and happy to have you back.

The next time we snuck out, you practically flew toward the dock. I stumbled on a root, keeping up with you.

"Careful," you said as you caught me before I fell. "It's all fun and games until somebody turns up dead."

"Is that a rule?" I asked.

You squeezed my arm before letting go. "More like an observation."

"It's true that if either of us is in danger of tripping to death, it's me," I said. I was born clumsy.

You flashed me a grin. "Don't worry. I'll always catch you."

We settled in at the dock and when I heard the sound of footsteps, I froze, afraid we were caught, but you beamed and Jackson appeared on the path, with Nitin behind him.

"Were you expecting company?" I asked, but the answer was clear. Jackson dropped beside you with a "Hey, babe" and Nitin shrugged apologetically before sitting down to close the circle. I tried to stare some sense into you, but you let all opinions except Jackson's roll right off you.

Soon you and he slipped off down the path for some privacy. Nitin had a pack of cards and we played Egyptian Rat Screw in the moonlight, keeping our slaps light and stealth, chasing the cards whenever they blew. We completed three full rounds before you returned, and not quick ones. When I was distracted, we were evenly matched.

I was exhausted the next day. Exhausted and grumpy.

You were floating. Jackson was insufferable. I decided this time I would stay out of it. There was no use wasting my breath talking sense into you when clearly you didn't want to hear it. I would save my energy for when he dumped you again and you needed me.

It didn't take long.

That guy was so damn predictable. Weren't you bored by the repetition?

Now everyone thinks they know all about how the jealousy burned in your gut until you flared up and couldn't take it, and on the next-to-last night, you killed him. Killed him for being a flirt. Killed him for choosing his girlfriend. Killed him for being careless with your heart.

Honestly, Lainie, there are nights I wish I could believe that too.

Dr. Rita found that interesting. "You'd rather believe she snapped and killed him than that he dove in shallow water and hit his head on a rock? Tell me more about that."

"Not really," I mumbled. "But at least it would mean she stood up for herself."

"You see her as a victim here. First Jackson's victim, and now a victim, a target, of the police."

"I guess so," I agreed, to get her off my back and be allowed to change the subject sooner. I've started hating talking to Dr. Rita about you. She doesn't get it. I can't explain you. She keeps twisting it all wrong.

Jackson was like a pebble in your shoe that for some reason you refused to shake out. That's not being a victim, it's making a bad choice. A temporary one. Even if you walked for miles with it, it wouldn't destroy you. You'd be fine and forget it once the pebble was finally gone, whether you came to your senses and got rid of it or it bounced out on its own.

That's how it should have been. You should have dumped him and kept walking.

The idea that you killed him in a fit of uncontrolled passion is laughable. Ironic, even. Because even at your most upset, you were always in control of your reactions. When you allowed yourself to rage at him, it was just that—you *allowed* it. You never let your guard down fully with others. Not in public, and not with Jackson. Only with me.

They got Teflon Lainie. When something stuck to you, it was because you let it. You were never unprepared or unhinged.

If you were to kill someone, it would be cold-blooded. Premeditated.

Don't worry, I would never tell the cops that.

Haha?

Love,
Kayla

Camper and Counselor Interviews, Statements, and Posts
August 14–November 24

"Lainie killing Jackson was, like, a *thing*. An inside joke or something. I don't know. I'm not sure when it started, but it happened all the time. Like, they'd be walking toward each other across the green and Lainie would cock her finger like a gun and make a clicking sound with her tongue, and Jackson would flail his arms and fall dramatically, or clutch his chest and stumble over, or act like half his face had been blown off. Or at dinner or campfire she'd lean over and say 'bang bang,' and he'd die. It seemed silly at the time, but it's creepy now, looking back."

"This one time I was sitting with Kayla and Lainie at breakfast. Not *with* them, but at their table, I guess. And they were talking, quietly at first, but pretty soon it got louder, about all the ways they would like to kill Jackson. Not real ways, I didn't think at the time, but gross stuff. Things like skinning him alive or roasting him like a marshmallow or suffocating him with his own balls. It was sick. They were giggling and Lainie kept glaring over at him and Emma—they were together for, like, a minute, so I guess that was why. But it was really gross. And disturbing. I wish I'd said something to someone then. I didn't think she would actually do it. But I definitely think she was capable. That stuff she said . . . I think she really hated him then, even though they got back together."

"There was a night in July when a bunch of us played Assassin, and they were in my group. Kayla was Moderator and she chose Jackson as Assassin, and Jackson killed Lainie, and all of us guessed it immediately because of course he did. And after it was out there, Lainie was like, 'Then I rose from the dead and killed you back! Now we're both gone, like Romeo and Juliet.' And Jackson grabbed her around the middle and said, 'My ghost too shall have revenge!' And Kayla grumbled, 'Romeo and Juliet killed themselves, not each other,' but Jackson and Lainie were too busy making out to notice, and everyone thought they were adorable.

"I keep thinking about that and getting chills. Has anyone else mentioned it?"

October 4

Dear Lainie,

My dad is making stir-fry and the whole house smells like garlic—a smell that always and forever will remind me of you, and the time we got stuck on kitchen duty and Chef Beverly made us peel a thousand garlic cloves. I'm convinced my hands still smell of it, though not nearly as much as they did in the days after. Chef Beverly was a sadist. (Seriously, *do* they run background checks on the people they hire at camps?) That was cruel and unusual punishment. Though, okay, it was also kind of fun.

Oh god, do you remember before then, in the first or second week, when on our way to the dock we heard A SOUND and thought for sure we'd be caught? Your arm shot out to stop me, and we crouched, frozen in place for eight centuries (it felt that long to my screaming, cramped-up legs), hyperventilating, as someone emerged from the faculty cabins, went up the hill, and disappeared behind the mess hall. They crossed right in front of us, maybe twenty feet away— one slight turn and their flashlight would have beamed directly at us. I understood then how a rodent feels the moment before it dies from fright.

(I found a mouse in our kitchen sink once, all stiff and dead and belly-up. My mom said it probably fell in there, couldn't get out, and panicked and gave itself a heart attack. Poor mousy.)

But we were safe, and when the danger passed, we continued to the lake, high on our second chance at life. We guessed it must have been Chef Beverly on her way to the kitchen—searching for Scooby Snacks, you joked, and I honestly thought that was some kind of junk food, like gummy bears or Teddy Grahams.

I was like, "Do you think she has a stash of Goldfish in there too? I need to get my parents to send me some. Wouldn't those taste so good right now?"

You patted me on the head and said, "You are the cutest thing I've ever met. Never change," and it took me a minute to understand that Scooby Snacks aren't snacks at all but some kind of drug (though exactly what kind of drug, you didn't seem to know for sure, either).

(Okay, the internet tells me it's either pot, mushrooms, or Valium, or maybe "club drugs," whatever that means. Maybe drugs to take when you go dancing? See, even when I try to delve into edgy rebelliousness, I can't help but stay hopelessly innocent.)

I was never embarrassed about stuff like that when it happened in front of you. Your delight was always worth it. I kind of played it up sometimes, it's true, but it was a joke between us. One that soured and stopped feeling funny whenever Jackson was around. You never made me feel embarrassed about being naïve, but Jackson was a jackass. And although you didn't make it worse, you also didn't make it better.

Tiny sad violin

I didn't have to peel all that garlic, please remember. You got in trouble for coming in three minutes after curfew two nights in a row, but you weren't out with me—you were sucking face outside our cabin with Jackson, and couldn't pull yourself off him in time.

Why Jackson didn't get in trouble when he must have shown up at his cabin even later than you got to ours, I don't know, but I guess his counselor looked the other way or didn't notice. "Boys will be boys" or whatever. I think you wanted him to step up and turn himself in, but when he heard you got kitchen duty, he just said, "That sucks," and let you take the fall alone. So I went with you.

Instead of going to free swim or archery, or back to the cabin to read, I walked you to the kitchen to report for your punishment, and when Chef Beverly looked us up and down and said, "Two of you?" I said, "Yup," and shrugged when you whispered, "You don't have to do that."

She tossed us aprons and bandannas for our hair and said, "Okay, troublemakers. I hope you like the smell of garlic because you'll be reeking of it all week." It was only a slight exaggeration.

(I still can't figure out how Chef Beverly always smelled like cigarettes when there was no smoking anywhere on campus and no one ever saw her light up. Did she have a secret lair? Sneak deep into the woods to do it? Not smoke all summer but still stink from years of nicotine residue coming out her pores? *Quel mystère.*)

The garlic did reek, and it stung in a cut I hadn't realized I had on my finger. But sitting on a stool beside you, peeling clove after clove and dropping them into a big white bucket, while Chef Beverly sang off-key to endless country tunes on the radio—chopping and gesturing with her alarmingly enormous knife—those were some of my favorite few hours of camp. First, you were infinitely grateful, and I felt like some kind of friendship superhero for making what was, really, a pretty small sacrifice on my part. Second, we were in it together, just as we should be, the way things hadn't always felt between us since you'd gotten distracted by Jackson.

While we peeled, we talked about which campers we thought the counselors secretly couldn't stand and why (Chef Beverly's face gave nothing away, but I'm sure we were right), and what superlatives we would give everyone if we were creating a camp yearbook. I let you declare yourself and Jackson "Cutest Couple" (but only since Rach and Melanie weren't official yet), and blushed when you assigned me "Most Random" and "Most Loyal." We pinned "Biggest Flirt" on Jackson—though you weren't thrilled about it—and chose "Most Likely to Win a Nobel Prize" for Nitin, though we disagreed over a Nobel Prize in what. (Peace! Obviously peace.) I wanted to give you "Most Likely to Win an Oscar" or "Most Unforgettable," but you insisted on "Best Sneeze," and it's true that yours is the weirdest and most surprising sneeze I have ever heard. "Sneeze Most Likely to Win an Oscar," I suggested, and you liked that.

When the bucket of garlic was half-full, you lifted your chin, wrinkled your nose, and declared, "This song pisses me off."

I hadn't been listening to the music at all. I tuned in long enough to catch the chorus: something about a man deciding to shoot his wife when he finds out she's been cheating.

"Why?" I asked. It seemed no worse than the other songs Chef Beverly had been playing.

"It's offensive," you said. "The whole idea of a crime of passion makes me furious. It's such bullshit."

"You don't believe in crimes of passion?" You held stances on things I'd never thought to think about.

"I don't believe in passion as an excuse for violence against women, no," you said, chucking another naked clove into the bucket. "It perpetuates the idea that it's understandable and *normal* when a woman is beaten or killed by a man who is just so passionate he can't control himself when her choices tick him off. Adultery is not an excuse for murder. It doesn't make beating your wife more okay."

You stared me down, but I wasn't about to dispute that.

"Men love putting the blame for their anger and violence on the very people they're beating or killing. They act like it's natural or even noble and romantic to get caught up in the moment and want to kill us—like, how could we expect any different? It's our fault." Your hands flew through the air as you spoke, sending garlic skins skittering in all directions. "We provoked them to kill or beat us because we cheated, just like we provoke them to rape or grope us by flirting or existing, and drive them to distraction by what we wear to school, and cause them to hate us as politicians or people by being too aggressive or too demanding or too needy or too shrill or too *anything* outside the box they want us to stay in."

You looked ready to burst into flame. "Like, why should they have to consider us to be full people, with internal lives and needs and desires just as valid as theirs? Women are objects. Of course you get mad and lash out at or destroy your object when it frustrates and betrays you. Who can blame you? How infuriating. It shouldn't have misbehaved. We should look pretty—but not too pretty—and shut up and smile and be grateful and stay in our place and agree with the mens," you raged.

Across the kitchen, Chef Beverly gave a slow clap. We glared at her. "Amen, sister," she said. "Amen." She beheaded a clump of carrots with her knife.

When the bucket was full and your punishment paid, we scrubbed our hands with soap and the lemon halves Chef Beverly said might help, but which mostly made me yelp when the juice seeped into my finger cut. "Out, damned stench," you muttered as you washed, and I wiggled my fingers in your face. "At least now we can repel vampires with our fingertips," I said, and you agreed that would definitely be useful.

But instead the garlic repelled Jackson. "You stink," he said, sniffing the air and pushing you away when you wrapped yourself around him in the food line. You acted like that was fine. Cool as ever. But the light in your eyes flickered.

"At least it's our fingers, not our breath," I said.

He kissed you, as if to check. "Thank god."

You pulled away, perhaps inspired by your own rant. "Don't worry, boys, we won't bother you with our stench. Kayla and I have urgent business on the other side of the room. Ta-ta."

I shrugged at Nitin, who said, "I kind of like it." I lifted my tray and followed you to a table full of girls. My heart was full.

I knew you were capable of standing up to him. I admit I loved you best when you did.

Ugh, okay, the stir-fry must be ready because Adele is calling me to set the table for dinner. I got a pass from stuff like that for a while, but Dr. Rita thinks it's a good idea for us to "restore normalcy as much as possible" and "move on with living" even as you're stuck in limbo, awaiting your trial. They're taking her word as gold (maybe because it costs about as much), so here I go. Normal, normal, normal. Whatever that is now. (Apparently it's chores. And actually doing my homework.)

Wish you were here.

Love,
Kayla

P.S. If I could take the fall with you for Jackson's death, would you want me to? Peeling garlic together for the next twenty years to life?

Maybe I'm glad you can't answer that.

P.P.S. I wonder if Chef Beverly thought about telling that story to the police . . . or if she had, if it might have given them pause or changed their minds about your motive or whatever.

Maybe, like me, she told them just the bare minimum—only what I truly had to.

Maybe they never interviewed the cook.

P.P.P.S. If this were Clue, you would definitely be Miss Scarlett—sultry, cunning, elusive. I'm thinking that makes me Colonel Mustard—especially the grumpy whiskers.

Wouldn't it be great if this were just a game? If an envelope revealed the answers, then we set it all up and played again?

It was Chef Beverly, with the knife, in the kitchen! And next time Nitin, with the rock, in the cabin! No need for motives, juries, evidence, or confessions—the proof's right there in the cards!

And then we'd escape through our own secret passageway.

P.P.P.P.S. Maybe Dr. Rita's right, maybe I am still in denial a little. And, okay, Adele is going to burst a blood vessel if I don't go set the table right now. *Mothers.*

October 8

Dear Lainie,

Last night I dreamed we were out on the dock with the sun on our backs and our toes in the lake, and everything was good and right with the universe. There were other campers swimming in an area nearby and we could hear their shouts and splashes, but they weren't with us. We were in our own private bubble, just the two of us, intimate and close, and I felt connected and happy and content.

Then it was nighttime. The swimmers were gone and the moon was out and we'd been so wrapped up in talking, we'd stayed out past dinner, past campfire, past curfew. I stood in the blue darkness, worried we'd get in trouble, but you pulled me back down and assured me it was fine. I sat, but I couldn't focus anymore. I felt anxious. When I looked at the water, it was thick with blood.

"Stop overreacting," Dream You said. "It's nothing. The water's always like that."

I wasn't certain you were wrong, but I felt uneasy. I tried to convince you we should go. "Like this?" you taunted, and you kicked your feet, churning and splashing. Your squeals were playful until they turned into screams.

Jackson's corpse floated up through the frothy, bloody water. You kicked him back down, but he bobbed like an apple. You tried again and again. Nothing would sink him.

"Just leave him. Let's go," I said. I held out my hand. "Please."

You turned on me. "You wanted this," you hissed.

"No," I said.

"You wanted this and you're glad he's dead and that's why you didn't try to save him." You were hysterical, swinging your arms wildly. I stepped back, but I wanted to step closer. "Look what you did!" you shrieked. "Look what you made us do! I would never have done this without you! You wanted it! You caused it! I know you're the reason this happened!"

"No no no no no no no," I repeated until I woke up crying and sweating.

Thinking about it now, I'm shaking again.

I never wanted it to happen, Lainie. Truly, truly I didn't. I know it was only a dream, but I still want you to believe me.

Dr. Rita says everyone we encounter in our dreams is some version of ourself. So I guess I'm the corpse and I'm you and I'm me, and I blame myself and know I'm innocent and want to push the body back down.

Yeah.

That seems about right.

Love,
Kayla

October 12

Dear Lainie,

Dr. Rita thinks I need to be more honest with myself and acknowledge my frustration and anger with you for the way things are now. She says it's natural that I would feel some resentment for what I'm going through, and even though it's "admirable and understandable" that I want to protect and defend you, I'm "not doing anyone any favors" by "keeping it all bottled up," and I "won't truly feel safe or be able to fully heal" until I "allow a place for those kinds of thoughts and emotions to exist."

Adele and Peter are paying her $275 an hour to dole out that advice, two sessions a week, so here goes.

I feel sad that I've lost you.

You know that one already.

I'm disappointed that what happened with Jackson came between us, when it should have only brought us closer.

I'm disappointed you didn't tell me everything—that the morning after, caught up in grief, you didn't confide in me, didn't confess or explain or even create more lies to tell me. I was there for you, but you didn't need me. Not the way you should have. I'm disappointed you didn't trust me with everything that happened to you with him.

I'm mad at myself—and at you—for the way that made me question you. Not out loud, but in my heart. Just for a moment. But that moment mattered. I can't take it back. I'm angry about the damage it caused.

I'm hurt that you gave me reason to doubt you. I'm hurt you gave me reason to doubt *us*. And I resent it too. It so easily could have not been this way, if only you'd trusted me like before.

I resent that it all went so fast, and the speed and the shock and the blur and confusion meant we got separated before we could work this through and figure it out. All summer, you could always make things better for me, and I always made things better for you, and we talked out everything. Together. I feel cheated we didn't do that in the end.

I'm scared about the future.

I feel abandoned by you, and a little betrayed. You're not here for me right now. I still need my best friend, but you've left me, even if leaving me wasn't your intention.

You must be allowed to make phone calls from jail. Why haven't you called or written?

I know why.

I'm sure your lawyer told you not to. But you've never let anyone stop you from going after what you want before this. So maybe you don't want to see me. Maybe you don't want me back. Even after all we went through.

I'm scared and mad that I'm on my own, and I feel helpless that I can't really be there for you, either. Helpless and hopeless and also beside the point.

I feel foolish that you're still central to me, still the only person I really want to talk to, but to you I'm now secondary at best. Or maybe I'm nothing. A blip in the memory bank. A slideshow you never replay, because you're focused on too many other, more important things. That's my deepest, darkest worry, though of course it's not true. Is it?

I'm angry that in the end, you chose Jackson over me. That's a twisted way to see it, perhaps, but I feel that way and it hurts. It hurts that you were so focused on him, you didn't think about the damage you might cause to us. It makes me furious, and that fury makes me crumple with guilt and hurt more.

I'm angry you were careless with both our hearts.

I'm frustrated that I can't feel angry at you for long. Sadness floods in quickly. A million other emotions too.

But what good is being angry? It doesn't bring you back to me. It can't resurrect Jackson, or bury him for good. It doesn't change what happened, bring truth to light, or help me make sense of it, finally. It just makes me feel further from you. Lonelier.

Fuck this. It's not helping.

Love,
Kayla

P.S. On top of all this, I have a math test tomorrow. Are you glad that at least you're not in school? I wonder if someone brings you your homework. I wonder if you've figured out why $1 + 1 - 1 = 0$.

Camper and Counselor Interviews, Statements, and Posts
August 14–November 24

"Lainie and Kayla were the kind of friends who tell each other everything. If any of this was at all premeditated, you have to wonder how much Kayla knew."

"Of the two of them, Kayla was the calm and steady one—the straight man to Lainie's outrageousness. But it wasn't imbalanced. Kayla was Lainie's rock. She went along with Lainie's wild schemes but kept her grounded, for the most part. Without Kayla, Lainie might have just dived right off the deep end long before this. Kayla usually kept her from going too far."

"I remember seeing Kayla at campfire one night, just kinda staring into the distance with this look in her eyes like the light had gone right out of them. That was only a day or two before Jackson died. I thought at the time she was probably sad about the end of camp, like most of us were, but god, it could have been anything.

"I wonder what it's like for her now, and if she believes it's possible Lainie could have done it. I don't think so, most of the time. It's like, there has to be some other explanation. Someone else involved. But then I hear some of the things that people are saying and I don't know anymore. I just don't know."

"It didn't *look* like things changed when Lainie and Jackson got together, but Lainie did kind of ditch her sometimes, and I've been there. It stinks. When your best friend is with someone else, you're going to feel like a third wheel sometimes, no matter how hard they work to include you. Because that's the thing: It shouldn't have to be work. But it is. It's inherently imbalanced. Even if you haven't really been replaced, you've sort of actually been replaced, at least temporarily. And there's nothing to do besides wait it out. So I felt sorry for her, as her counselor. It had to be hard."

"I saw someone online saying Kayla was Lainie's rock, but I think she was more like Lainie's guard dog. The small, fierce kind with hyper-alert eyes, ready to growl and bare her teeth at anyone who came too close. Loyal and protective, and much more vicious than she looks. Like if she were to sink her teeth into your ankle, you'd have to saw through your own leg to get her off. Know what I'm saying?"

October 21

Dear Lainie,

I had a good session with Dr. Rita today. She helped me work through something that has been pricking at the back of my brain for a while but I haven't quite had the words to describe it. It's about the concept of identity, sort of, and the challenge of "reconciling multiple versions of the self," as Dr. Rita put it. It was surprisingly helpful to think it through out loud with her. Mostly it was a relief to hear she didn't think my questions were weird. She made me feel kind of smart for asking them.

I've been thinking a lot since camp about authenticity. About who really knows us, and how well we can truly know ourselves.

I know: deep thoughts. They're not completely random, though.

All summer I had this vague awareness that if the people who think they know me at home saw who I was at camp, they would probably barely recognize me. I was different there. I was different with you. But it wasn't fake or inauthentic. If anything, it was more real. There were no preconceived notions. I could just be who I was in that moment. Which was someone pretty different from who I'd been at home.

If where you are and who you're with and what you're doing and thinking about changes, how can something not change in you too? But I was still myself, of course. Wasn't I?

(Ugh, this is coming out just as convoluted as when I tried explaining it to Dr. Rita. Don't worry, there's more clarity later . . . I hope. But yeah, there's zero succinctness. Sorry.)

If Camp Me was the truest version of me but doesn't match who I'm able to be at home, why shouldn't the same be true of Camp You?

Yes, this philosophizing stems from trying to wrap my head around everything people have been saying about you online. I'm not supposed to go near it, but I can't stop lurking and scrolling and watching. It's addictive. And it's creepy in an uncanny valley way—like watching some kind of gossip-generated version of you. They've made a Frankenstein's monster of sewed-up, mismatched parts: a person who sort of moves like you and talks like you, and everyone says is you, but it's most definitely not you. Not the you that I know. I can't look away, and I want to run screaming in the other direction too. (You most definitely could go as yourself for Halloween this year and everyone would be instantly horrified, haha.)

But even though people from home would be surprised by who I was at camp, they wouldn't be able to point to a lie of it. There was no lie. It was just me being who I was, in those circumstances, with that best friend, who saw me as I most wanted to be and therefore allowed me to be that version of myself. It wasn't planned. It just *was*, in large part thanks to you.

You also had a version of yourself you wanted to be last summer. You had several versions.

Each of them felt purely *you*, at least to me. But I understood the performance. To people who didn't see and know the real you, the different versions seem full of contradictions. There are inconsistencies. Lies. And that's what's causing all this trouble now.

I'm the only one who saw your full truth. I still see it. I'm trying to keep holding it tight.

But truth can be slippery. Hard to look at straight-on. It's too open to interpretations and viewpoints.

Lies are more solid. Sometimes they feel more real.

Quick diversion, because it just popped into my head and I know you miss my randomness: Remember the night we played Truth or Truth? (Jackson complained about no dares, but you were right—truths are the good part.)

It was my turn to ask a question and I lobbed you an easy one: "If you could have any superpower, what would you choose?"

"Telekinesis," you answered immediately. "If I could move things with my mind, I wouldn't have to get off the couch to get snacks when I'm feeling lazy."

"And you could freak people out by making shit fly around the room. Think how great that would be in, like, gym class," Jackson said.

You barely glanced at him. "Yeah, I'd probably just use it for snacks."

You'd been kind of snippy with Jackson all evening, but he hadn't appeared to notice, which only made it worse. You two were "just friends" again due to an episode of guilt over Meghan that had hit Jackson hard that afternoon. I wasn't holding my breath that it would last.

You turned to Nitin. "Truth or truth?"

He grinned. "Truth."

"What's something nobody else at camp knows about you?"

Nitin shifted his weight. I wondered how you would answer the same question. "Well . . . no one knows it's my birthday," he said.

"What? *Today?*" I said. You and Jackson looked equally surprised.

"Yeah. As of midnight." It must have been around one a.m.

You swatted his knee. "You didn't tell us!"

Nitin shrugged, kind of cutely. "Actually, I just did."

You snort-laughed. "Did you just 'Well, actually' me?" He shrugged again. I hadn't realized he had this impish side. You shook your head and nudged him, almost flirting. "It's your birthday, so we'll let it slide."

"Are you sixteen or seventeen?" I asked.

It was dark, but I sensed his blush. "Fifteen," he admitted. He lowered those ridiculously long lashes.

Jackson leaned in. "No way. You're younger than us?"

"Only by a year," he mumbled.

Jackson started to say something, but you cut him off. "Nitin's an old soul. Fifteen going on forty." You leaned over and kissed him on the cheek. "Happy birthday," you said. He was practically glowing.

"Old soul," Jackson muttered, sour. You'd finally captured his attention. "What does that make me?"

You rolled your eyes. "You're an ass-soul. Obviously."

He smirked and I felt the heat switch back on between you. You'd be sucking face again by morning, I was sure.

"What am I?" I asked, hoping to pull you back to me.

You looked straight at me, your gaze a flare of starlight. "You're perfect. Never change."

But you'd already changed me.

Part of what I'm struggling with since the end of camp is that I feel like I lost not only you, but also the person I was with you. Camp Me. Randy. The best me. I wonder sometimes if I even *was* her, or if she's just a story you invented, brought to life. Because really, is there a *me* who could ever be that daring, bold, and brave without you? Now that you're gone, I'm nowhere near as funny or interesting.

Dr. Rita says I'm still plenty interesting (she has to; we're paying her) and the way I'm feeling makes sense: that a big part of who I was this summer was your best friend, and the loss of a defining friendship like ours (even under less traumatic circumstances) can leave one feeling adrift. It "can shake the foundation of who you are," which is why, she says, it's a risk to attach yourself to someone else. When someone you were leaning on steps or falls away, it's a struggle to regain your balance and relearn how to stand on your own. But that doesn't mean the person I was with you is lost completely.

Dr. Rita says she hopes that as I find stability within myself and continue to heal, I'll come to view the risks of leaning on someone again as ultimately worth it. That part of our work together is rebuilding my ability to trust, though that trust has been deeply betrayed.

I don't like to think of you as betraying me.

What happened between you and Jackson happened between you and Jackson. It had nothing to do with me. And yet . . . you let me down. I can admit that. Even if your worst crime was just being thoughtless, it still hurt me.

Dr. Rita says phrasing it that way to myself is real progress.

Woo-fucking-hoo.

Okay but here is a thing I keep spinning on: If you told me a string of tiny lies and I believed them . . . does that make our friendship untrue? What if they were lies you were telling yourself too?

I think you wanted to deceive yourself about Jackson, and to do that, you had to deceive me too. You didn't mean to hurt me. I was a casualty of your war with yourself. But that doesn't make my wounds less deep.

I think I still know you despite those lies. Maybe I know you better because of them.

But it depends on this: What else did you lie to me about? And why?

Love,

Kayla

October 22

Channel 5 News

"Jury selection began today in the second-degree murder case of Elaine Baxter, the alleged 'Summer Camp Slayer,' who is charged with the death of her on-again, off-again summer-camp sweetheart, Jackson Winter, whose body was found by a camp counselor in Jaspertown Lake on the shores of Camp Cavanick property in August. The jury selection process is expected to move swiftly, with opening statements set for November second, according to defense attorney Michael Desir, who gave a brief interview outside the courthouse this afternoon.

"Desir praised Judge Candice Rodriguez's decision not to allow news cameras inside the courtroom, saying Miss Baxter, who has entered a plea of not guilty, 'deserves a fair and impartial trial, not a media circus,' in which she will have the chance to prove 'once and for all her complete and total innocence' and 'finally be able to put this outrageous allegation behind her and fully mourn the tragic loss of Jackson Winter, who was her close friend.'"

"This story is doubly tragic for the two teenage lives being destroyed by it. Lainie Baxter is a sixteen-year-old girl guilty only of falling in love, and she is as devastated by Jackson Winter's death as she is innocent of it."

"Prosecutor Marsha Davis called the sentiment 'a pretty tale' and indicated she is confident the state's case against Baxter will prove otherwise.

"Much has been made in the press of the initial statement Elaine

Baxter gave to police on the morning Jackson Winter's body was found, claiming not to have seen him since they'd said goodnight at curfew the evening before. Baxter later retracted that statement and admitted to having snuck out of her cabin to meet Jackson by the lake after midnight—a rendezvous she claims ended with a last kiss around two o'clock in the morning, which is close to the time the coroner's report estimates as the time of his death.

"Prosecutor Davis has stated on record in the past that Elaine Baxter, quote, 'is a known liar who, by her own admission, lied to police in her initial statement about the circumstances surrounding Jackson Winter's death, and, the state will prove, has been lying about it ever since,' end quote."

October 31

Dear Lainie,

Here's something I don't know about you, that I suddenly wish I could ask: What's your favorite Halloween candy? Don't say candy corn, please, or it will change everything I think I know about you. I'm picturing you loving something weird, like Dots or Smarties (which, I learned tonight, are called Rockets in Canada. Not that I was in Canada. Just collecting random facts as usual).

Mine is Mounds, followed by peanut-butter cups, followed by little boxes of Junior Mints. I'm also down with Nerds, lollipops, and malted milk balls—but no Tootsie Rolls, candy corn, or other sugary wax masquerading as edible. I won't stand for it.

Adele and Peter gave out KitKats this year. If you were here, I would split this one with you, but instead I'll have to eat both halves myself. Nom nom. Adele wore her witch hat and a fake nose (long, warty) to answer the door to trick-or-treaters, and Peter sported Harry Potter glasses that might as well have been regular glasses, since he wasn't wearing the rest of the costume. They made an enormous bowl of buttered popcorn and seemed stunned, then delighted, to learn I wouldn't be joining them for a movie marathon after dinner. (No slashers or murder mysteries in the queue this year. My parents are nothing if not tasteful.) Instead, I went to a party.

I'm invited to parties now, apparently, although I never go. But I accidentally mentioned this one to Dr. Rita when telling her about

Dina Who I Usually Have Lunch With (which is exactly how I think of them, I guess to avoid having to use the word *friend*. I don't know if they're my friend, exactly, though I think they probably want to be, and we maybe act like we're friends, in that we sit together regularly and talk about our lives and don't dislike each other or anything, so maybe they think that's what we are already. I don't know. It's not like it was with you. And I'm not sure I'm really ready to have another friend—definitely not a best friend—though I haven't straight-up told them that. We've only been eating together a few weeks). They invite me to stuff outside of school sometimes, and usually I say no, but sometimes I'll agree to hang out for a while and do homework together or whatever. When they mentioned this party, I said I probably wouldn't go, but for some reason I told Dr. Rita about it. She thought it would be good for me to get out, be social, make friends. Distract myself from the impending trial.

Replace you, she meant, but of course you can't be replaced.

I told Dina Who I Usually Have Lunch With I might go with them after all, and they said "cool" and that it was fine if I didn't want to wear a costume, but they would bring me some wings or something just in case. Which turned out to be great because otherwise I would have been the only one not dressed up, and *not* wearing wings and the glitter I let Dina dab on my cheeks would have made me stick out and seem awkward.

High school is strange.

The party wasn't bad. I felt self-conscious at first, especially when Dina started talking to some kids I don't know and didn't feel like being introduced to because I hate standing around on the edge of a group I don't belong in. I'd rather just stand by myself. I wandered into the kitchen and kept my chin up and my shoulders back, trying to look confident and at ease—the way you used to stand—and poured myself some punch. I imagined I was you while I sipped it, looking around to see who was there, and pretty soon I started to relax. I remembered that all summer, I'd fit in.

I poured more punch and walked into the living room, where Dina waved from across the room. They were dressed as a cereal comma, with a punctuation mark cut from a Honey Nut Cheerios box taped to their button-down shirt. In between us people were dancing and as I watched, I found myself moving my head and hips to the music, and realized I felt kind of fuzzy-warm and happy, like my brain was a furry little animal—like silly, funny Ollie had moved in to live in my skull—and everything at the party looked softer and happier too. A little blurry if I moved too fast, but that was fun.

I put my cup down and danced for real. This guy Ian from my math class grabbed my hand and twirled me around, and I twirled him back, and the music got faster. We dipped and the world spun, and I borrowed his hat and touched my own cheek, then his, to loan him some of Dina's glitter. Now I was a pirate fairy and he was a boy who sparkled.

We went outside to get some air, and I flirted the way I'd seen you flirting: a tip of the head, a quirk of the lips. A gaze held and released. An inviting laugh. A touch on the arm. Why not? It was Halloween. You're not supposed to go as yourself.

When people asked what I was dressed as, I changed the answer each time—Tinker Bell, the Tooth Fairy, a dragonfly, a mosquito—but in truth my costume was you. I was the Summer Camp Slayer, but before. Before things turned bloody. Before it went bad. When it was still all glitter and charm and the magic of make-believe.

Your trial starts in two days (or tomorrow, technically, since it's currently 2 a.m.) but you're already being tried in the court of public opinion. It's not unanimous—I'm still voting not guilty—but All the World's a Jury and they're pretty convinced by the evidence.

It's hearsay, mostly. The stories. The lies. Speculation on the part of those who knew you, or sort of did. (Emma, in particular, will not shut up. She still wants a slice of your spotlight. Nitin, like me, hasn't made a single public comment. Jackson, of course, isn't talking.) But your DNA was all over him—your skin cells under his fingernails—too much to wash away in the lake. Some say that's the sign of a struggle, that the DNA got there when he was fighting you off. That the cops should have checked you for scratches.

I know you had scratches.

I can picture it so clearly: the two of you in the midnight dark, his hands running up and down your arms and back, all over your tingling skin. His nails raking gently, then digging in, as his kisses, too, varied in intensity. Some scratches were featherlight, and others harder, like the ones I gave Ian as we kissed outside the party tonight, experimenting. How far was too far?

My nails sank in and Ian pulled away. "Whoa there, tiger."

"Meow," I said, though cats don't have wings or glitter cheekbones. He came back for another kiss and my fingers roamed more lightly. Teasing. It was cold out, but his mouth was warm.

Was that what it was like being Jackson, kissing you? I don't think so because I didn't feel fireworks.

Remember the Fourth of July?

It was only the end of the second week, but already we'd been at Camp Cavanick forever. Life *before* felt impossibly far away and irrelevant. There was no reason to even think of an after. Six more weeks of perfect summer stretched before us.

We sat on the grassy hill, facing the lake, our abandoned paper plates at our sides. Other campers were all around us, but distant. Tossing a Frisbee in the last remnants of dusk; confiding secrets by the campfire; lounging in groups or pairs on the hillside like us.

When the sky was almost black, the first fireworks went off with a boom and crackle that echoed across the water. Everyone hushed. You slapped a mosquito on your leg and leaned your head against my shoulder. We watched. I'd never gotten the big deal about fireworks before, but these ones felt magical. Spectacular. I remember thinking, *This is really my life*, and being glad of it.

"Have you ever been in love?" you asked.

"Like, in *love* in love?" I asked.

You lifted your head and my shoulder felt cold. "Yeah."

I had never even been kissed. "I don't think so." You waited, so I went on. "I was kind of in love with my fourth-grade teacher, Ms. Henry," I said. You smiled. "And I had an embarrassingly huge crush on my brother's friend Jascha for a while, but I'm not sure either of those counts. Have you?"

The glow of the next firework reflected off your face. "No. I thought I was, last spring. This girl Jasmine I went out with for a while. She was in my homeroom. We hooked up at the Valentine's dance. But now I think it wasn't love, exactly. I liked her a lot, but there weren't any fireworks. More like ... fireflies. We kind of flickered in and out, until it stayed out. There was never any huge, like, *passion*."

"Oh," I said.

You shifted. "What did you like about Jascha?"

I thought about it. "He was kind. Much kinder than anyone else I know. Just ... thoughtful."

He must have known about my crush on him, and it clearly wasn't mutual, but he was always sweet to me anyway, right up until he left for college. I haven't seen him since. "What did you like about Jasmine?"

"She smelled good." I laughed. You shrugged. "Pheromones, I guess. But mostly I liked how much she liked me."

I felt sad for Jasmine then, and weirdly a little triumphant.

But here's the thing: I don't think there was a Jasmine. Am I right?

Everyone you've ever made out with—or allegedly made out with, because no way could your mouth have been that busy—has emerged from the woodwork since the news about Jackson broke. Clearly some of those guys, if not all of them, made it up for the attention, or they're confusing their own fantasies with reality. Your supposed sexual history is a topic of national discussion. But there has been no mention of Jasmine.

I've scoured every photo I can find of you, and of parties you might have attended, searched the accounts of everyone you were friends or friendly or acquainted with in the spring of last year. There doesn't seem to have been a girlfriend. There doesn't seem to be anyone at your school named Jasmine. And I can't for the life of me figure out why you would have lied about it. Lied to *me*.

Maybe Jasmine was a nickname you gave her, like Randy. But my gut says that isn't it.

Maybe someday, when this is over, I'll get to hear an explanation. Maybe you'll offer me one that's real.

A week or so after the Fourth, you found fireworks with Jackson. I don't know how it felt when you kissed him, but I know the rest was plenty explosive. I guess that's what you wanted, and I guess I should have known—you'd straight-up told me so, hadn't you? But I didn't understand it in that moment. I thought you meant something else.

Me kissing Ian tonight wasn't like you kissing Jackson. It was closer to me kissing you—or to you kissing me, to be more accurate—but without the audience. And with less shitty motivations. Still, I was using him with those kisses, just like you tried to use me.

I don't think he minded.

You know what it felt like when you kissed me the first time? It felt like falling. Not in a good way. It felt like we'd been gliding along, flying high, and you shoved me out of the airplane with no warning, no parachute, just a gentle laugh and a slip of tongue. Your lips were soft on mine, but what I felt was my insides plummeting.

Still, I kissed you back. By then I was so accustomed to going along with your performances, I had no way to react besides playing along. Nitin looked away and Jackson basically salivated—which was the purpose, wasn't it. You kissed me in front of Jackson, *for* Jackson, to prove some point that had nothing to do with me. I had always been your sidekick and coconspirator, but in that moment I was only your prop.

You knew it was a mistake. You were extra good to me in the days after, extra present in a way you mostly hadn't been since thoughts of Jackson had hijacked your brain. You never apologized with words, but I forgave you. It was a quick, thoughtless moment, and friends forgive each other those all the time. No harm done.

The second time was more confusing. It wasn't in front of Jackson. We had no audience, but still, I felt heavily aware of your awareness of him. The audience was implied, though not present.

That kiss lingered longer, and I felt it and tasted it. I wasn't falling. But it ended with a thud.

Did you feel it too? I pulled away and you opened your eyes and they seemed to brim over with questions. I shook my head and tried to answer one. "I just feel like that isn't what you want," I said. *You'd* kissed *me*, yet somehow I was the one left explaining. "You shouldn't kiss me unless you mean it," I added. I wasn't sure I wanted you to kiss me even then.

It hadn't occurred to either of us to think about me.

"Who says I don't mean it?" you asked, and I was quiet, because you'd made it worse. You grew flirtatious, defensive. "Can't it just mean kissing is fun?" Like how you would have said it to anyone. Anyone who didn't matter.

This wasn't what I'd thought our friendship was about.

"Don't do this." I was honest with you, and I wanted you to be honest back. "Don't use me for revenge, or as bait to lure him back to you. Don't pull me into it like that. It isn't fair."

I felt the motion of the dock on the tiny, lapping waves, and focused on the lake's unsteady rhythms. My vision blurred and I did not look at your face.

"I'm sorry," you said. "You're right. I won't do it again."

I didn't move.

"I've been a shitty friend. You deserve better."

I lunged and squeezed you in the tightest hug, but was the wetness on our cheeks from your tears or mine? I'm not certain. You squeezed back and we laughed, like that tornado of emotions was funny. Was there any disappointment mixed into your relief? It's a blur for me. I don't know what I felt.

That was only five days before the end.

I disentangled from Ian tonight when Dina came to find me, and dismissed him with a quick "See you in math." My lips felt numb from overuse.

I stumbled a little as we walked inside. Dina caught me by the arm. "Have you been drinking?" they asked.

I straightened their bow tie. "No." I hiccupped. "Only punch."

They looked at me with concern, and like they weren't sure if I was kidding.

"What?" I said, then "... Oh," as I realized my mistake.

"Wait. What did you think Booooooozy Poison Punch meant?" they asked.

"I thought they were just . . . words. Halloween words. You know . . . *boo. Poison.*"

You would have laughed, but for some reason Dina apologized. I guess they felt responsible. They made me drink two cups of water and eat some saltines they found in a cabinet before guiding me out to their car.

"Come on, let's get you home safe. Or do you want to come over so your parents don't see you? My dad wouldn't care."

I assured them my parents never see me anyway.

I don't know why I haven't told you about Dina before. I guess I didn't want you to think you're being replaced, because you're not. But it's not only that. (Obviously not. I do understand you don't read these letters before I delete them. I'm not that far gone.) My life at school and at home, when I'm not writing to you or reading about you online, feels so separate from you and *us* and camp. That gets truer every day, and I can't lie: It's a relief. It's a relief that there's another normal. That, with time, my brain has found things to think about other than you.

It's a relief, but I also hate it. I hate it because it feels like abandonment. Betrayal.

You don't get to move on from Camp Cavanick yet. It feels unfair sometimes that I do—like just by the fact of my life moving forward, against my will, I am somehow being disloyal to you. "Survivor's guilt," Dr. Rita calls it. That sounds like an oversimplification to me, but whatever.

Despite the guilt, I think you'd be proud of me (if also jealous). A party. The dancing. My first drinks. My first drunkenness. A sort-of friend. My first kisses with someone who isn't you.

This little fairy had an eventful Halloween.

Trick or treat?

Love,
Kayla

November 2

Maplewash County Post-Gazette

THE JURY HEARD OPENING STATEMENTS MONDAY IN the trial of Elaine Baxter, the sixteen-year-old who stands accused of killing her sometimes boyfriend, Jackson Winter, at the teen camp where they met last summer.

Prosecutor Marsha Davis told jurors she expected witnesses would describe Elaine Baxter, known as "Lainie," as "behaving erratically" in the days leading up to the morning of August 14, when Jackson Winter's body was recovered from Jaspertown Lake along Camp Cavanick property, hours after he apparently suffered a fatal blow to the head. "Over the course of this trial, a picture will unfold," Davis claimed, of Baxter as a "charismatic, beautiful, and seemingly fun-loving teenager" who is "deeply troubled and deceitful" beneath her appealing surface.

The prosecution promised to establish a pattern of Baxter's alleged "untrustworthy" behavior and submit "relevant evidence" that she has "a disturbing history of elaborate deceptions," "lying for fun," and "obsessive, jealous behavior exhibited toward Jackson Winter before his death."

Davis ended her opening statement by telling jurors they would hear testimony that Baxter's own initial statements given to police officers the morning after Winter's body was found, were "by her own later admission, fully misleading and untrue," and "clearly reveal that, that morning, Elaine Baxter had something significant to hide."

Baxter's defense attorney, Michael Desir, told jurors that the prosecution's case "is built on rumors and speculation." He urged jurors to pay close attention to the "actual facts and real evidence," and predicted the state would be "flailing" in its efforts to establish a reasonable motive for the alleged attack.

Desir acknowledged the defendant wasn't always "a perfect angel or even an ideal girlfriend," and that she sometimes "made things up out of regular teenage boredom" and "the normal and healthy adolescent temptation to push boundaries, and see what one can get away with." But that doesn't, he insisted, make her a murderer.

"What teenager hasn't at some point found themselves the subject of cruel, untrue rumors they'd be hard-pressed to disprove?" Desir asked, while reminding jurors, "We are trying this case in a court of law, not a high school hallway or an internet bubble." He ended his opening statement by saying, "The state must be held to a higher standard of proof. When pressed for real evidence, for hard facts that add up, their case will fall short—and you, the jury, will surely find the obvious choice is to acquit."

Jackson Winter's family sat quietly in the center of the courtroom throughout the opening statements. Their focus, a spokesman said later, was "on the enormous loss of their beloved son Jackson, who can never be returned to them, and their hope for the deliverance of justice."

Davis is set to begin presenting her case against Baxter when the trial resumes on Tuesday.

Camper and Counselor Interviews, Statements, and Posts
August 14–November 24

"I heard Lainie's lawyer wants Lainie to cry on the witness stand, so the jury will feel sorry for the poor pretty white girl."

"I heard the reason Lainie won't testify is if they put her on the stand, they can ask her under oath about all the other lies she told. Her lawyer doesn't want to open her up to that line of questioning."

"I heard when Jackson's body was found, Kayla begged Lainie not to speak to the police without a lawyer present."

"I heard the cops interviewed Kayla for over an hour that morning, and when her parents found out she'd been questioned with no supervision, they gave the camp director hell for letting that happen."

"I heard when Lainie got arrested, Kayla's lawyer had to stop her from confessing *she* killed him. The lawyer tried to scare her by saying false confessions are illegal, but she said 'good' because that way they'd be locked up together."

"I heard someone in Lainie's cabin saw her come back covered in blood, but Kayla burned Lainie's sheets and clothing to cover it up before anyone could find them."

"I heard someone in Emma's cabin noticed Emma's bed was empty after midnight."

"I heard the blood on Lainie's hoodie was from a nosebleed, not from Jackson. People will believe anything if it proves what they already think is true. It's so ridiculous. She didn't do it."

"I heard Kayla wouldn't tell the cops anything, and she still thinks Lainie is innocent."

"I heard Nitin told the cops he feels responsible for Jackson's death because he told Kayla some secret she must have told Lainie, one he didn't know Lainie didn't know already."

"I heard Lainie, Kayla, Nitin, and Jackson had a four-way orgy on the dock one night."

"I heard Lainie kissed Kayla in front of Jackson to make him jealous, and when he didn't seem to care, she totally lost it."

"I heard Kayla and Lainie made out one time, and when Jackson found out, he got violent and Lainie got scared."

"I heard Nitin stopped hanging out with them toward the end because he knew something like this was coming."

"I heard Nitin got grilled for, like, two extra hours, just because his skin is brown."

"I heard Jackson was blackmailing Chef Beverly, and she paid up because she couldn't afford to lose another job."

"I heard there was a weird guy passing through town—a skeezy drunk no one knew—and he was bragging about how he killed some kid at the camp. The police didn't bother to find him because they'd already decided to peg it on Lainie."

"I heard the defense will be calling Emma to the stand and demanding to know where she was during the murder."

"I heard Lainie was going to tell the girlfriend everything, so Jackson threatened her and she killed him in self-defense."

"I heard the first coroner's report said Jackson got the head injury from diving, but they got scared by the media coverage and changed it to say someone killed him."

"I heard she wanted to plead not guilty by reason of self-defense, but the lawyer said she had to just say not guilty."

November 5

Dear Lainie,

I've been thinking a lot about the fourth rule of crime: It Doesn't Matter What's True. It Only Matters What People *Think* Is True.

I wonder if you still believe that.

I wonder if you ever believed it, or if it's one of those things you said because it sounded good in the moment, then went with it because why not. You did have a habit of making shit up to amuse yourself, we both know. Though when I tried to argue this one, you made a convincing case.

"That's not true," I said.

"Of course it is." If I remember correctly, we were playing badminton—or rather, lazily bopping the little projectile thingy (oh my god, I just looked it up and it's called a *shuttlecock*) back and forth across the net with our rackets, since neither of us really knew how to play. (Though I guess it only matters that I *think* we were playing badminton, not whether it's true, haha.)

"What about money?" I pressed. "It doesn't matter if people think you have money—it only matters if you can afford to pay your bills." This was a loaded example to raise, I admit, since I knew you were at camp on full scholarship, and also knew I was the only one who knew it. You'd told me some things about your family's problems with money—your dad running up huge debt because he felt entitled to spend on whatever—and whoever—he wanted, while also being a tightwad at home. Your anger at your mom for letting him control way too much and not noticing what he'd done until it was far too late. Your exhaustion and worry over hearing them fight about that and everything else in their lives, until they stopped fighting and that felt worse. But I'd also witnessed how the impression you gave everyone else was that your family was loaded. I sort of understood the lie, but I was curious how you would explain it.

"No, that's a perfect example," you said. "If people think you have money, they one hundred percent treat you differently than if they think you're broke. Like, if the bank thinks you're rich, it's more likely to give you a loan. If other people think you're wealthy, they treat you with respect and authority—and if they think you're poor, they're more likely to look down on you. Shopkeepers follow you around if they think you can't buy things. Cops see you as criminal. People assume you're probably lazy or ignorant, even though poor people have to work harder than anyone else. It doesn't matter if you have money, because what matters in how they treat you is their perception."

"If the people are jerks," I said.

You shrugged. "Maybe. Or if they're human."

I wanted to argue against the injustice of that, but you didn't seem the least bit worked up.

"Or take the Dive and You'll Die legend," you continued. Emma and a friend walked past for the millionth time. For the millionth time, we ignored her. "It doesn't matter if it's true. People believe it, so it changes their behavior."

I snorted. "Except Jackson's."

You lunged for the shuttlecock (damn, I wish we'd known that word) and missed. "Nope, him too. You think he'd care about diving there if people didn't assume it was dangerous? There'd be no point if he wasn't showing off."

You were right, of course. Again.

Did you tell your lawyer that story, about the counselor who supposedly died when they dove off the dock into too-shallow water, on a long-ago drunken dare? That's something I did tell the cops. Not the legend, but the night we all discussed it—and how Jackson reacted when you brought it up.

He rolled his eyes. "They just tell us that to scare us. It's no realer than the ax murderer who lives in the woods."

For once I agreed with him. "Every camp needs an unhappy ghost to haunt it."

"And to teach us a valuable lesson on water safety," he added. "There's probably a ghost who died from running with scissors or not brushing their teeth down at the kiddie camp." I laughed, and a small moment of camaraderie passed between us.

Across the lake, a loon wailed, and Nitin shivered at the sound of it. You were tucked against Jackson, but you smiled at me. The loon calls were so eerie and beautiful at night. I loved that you loved them too.

"No, it's true. A counselor did drown after diving into the rocks," Nitin said. "My parents went to camp here—it's where they met—and they told me the story too."

You sat up. "Your parents knew the person who died?"

He snapped his gum, a dozen tiny rapid explosions. "No, they just heard about it. It was long before they were campers."

"Yeah, but if your parents were here thirty years ago, and they also heard it happened thirty years ago . . . ," I said. You nodded—we'd been thinking the same thing.

Nitin tilted his head. "Oh. Good point." I loved how Nitin, who got embarrassed about so many things, was never embarrassed to be wrong. Unlike Jackson, who would dig in harder on anything rather than admit he might be mistaken.

You peered over the edge, though the water was like ink. "I think you would have to dive from a place with more height. Or be incredibly unlucky," you said. "I mean, to actually die."

"Yeah, only a numbnut would dive straight into a rock," Jackson said. You giggled, but can we just admit right now he wasn't all that clever or funny? I'm sorry, I should be nice, the guy is dead, but *come on.*

"Still. I wouldn't try it," I said. But Jackson was already standing.

"As long as you don't dive at, like, ninety degrees, it's deep enough. Watch," he said. "I'll do it right now." He whipped off his shirt, which I assume was the point of that display of bravado, and you squealed and fussed and pulled him back down to you, and wrapped yourself around his bare torso.

Nitin and I stayed silent. The moment no longer involved us. You nibbled Jackson's shoulder and Jackson looked smug, like he'd proven or accomplished something. I never saw him dive in for real, but it wasn't the only time he mentioned it.

Jackson didn't take anything seriously. He walked through the world like he knew he could get away with whatever he wanted, and for the most part, he did. His default mode was the assumption he would be lucky, right up until his luck ran out.

He was exactly the kind of numbnut who would dive straight into a rock. Overconfidence plus entitlement should be bottled and sold as a drug. He definitely got high off it.

I don't know what's true about the Dive and You'll Die story. I'm starting to feel like I don't know what's true about anything anymore. If you were here, we would talk it through and you would make it make sense, and my head would stop spinning, finally.

Maybe.

Whatever you said, would I believe you? *Should* I? I'd still want to.

Here's where you're right, I guess, about the fourth rule: It doesn't matter anymore if you killed Jackson or not. It only matters what the jury believes.

Love,
Kayla

November 6

Dear Lainie,

I take it back. That was bullshit, the stuff I said about the fourth rule. It does matter what's true. It matters to me, anyway.

But what even *is* truth? Because we all have different perceptions and those perceptions shape our truths, and two contradicting things can be true at once, and argh and ugh and so forth.

Plus with something like love, friendship, or memories . . . those aren't tangible, provable things. They exist in our heads and hearts, and perceptions there are everything. So how does one determine the truth of them?

Your perceptions of your relationship with Jackson probably differed a lot from his (which differed still from mine, Nitin's, Emma's, or anyone else's), but that doesn't mean either of you was wrong, just that no one could have the full picture. Which I guess brings us back to your original hypothesis, and I can picture you smirking and raising your eyebrows like "See?"

But there is a true story of how Jackson died, even if perceptions of why are all different. Even if multiple whys might be true. And that story must matter, because if it weren't true, he wouldn't be dead. Right?

Excuse me a moment. [*Screams into the void*] *Brain explodes*

I hate working through impossible questions like this on my own now, without you—or with only the you in my head. It was so much better bullshitting out loud together. If we could meet on the dock and hash this all out, it would feel like we were solving the puzzle of the universe, not turning my brain to mush just trying to assemble the pieces.

It must be cold out on the dock now. Probably windy and frigid, like it is here today. That seems appropriate on the one hand and strange to imagine on the other. In my heart, it's endless summer there. A place we can never return to but that would always welcome us back. I guess the leaves are gone too. And any last trace of his blood.

Here's a complicated truth, and one I forget sometimes in the After, because it no longer fits with what I want to believe, but: Jackson was my friend too, in a way.

There's an alternate path this all might have taken, if the police had stuck to their original theory and declared Jackson's death an accident. A version of the After where instead of shoving us apart, his death would bring us closer together. Where there would be no arrest and no trial, no blame to throw around, and we would mourn and remember him together.

We would reach out sometimes just to say things like, "Remember the time he kept saying 'beignet' when he meant 'bidet,' and we all thought it was a story about washing his butt with a pastry, and you laughed so hard you nearly wet your pants?" Or, "Sometimes I picture the dimple that appeared on his right cheek whenever he was about to say something ridiculous, and I don't know whether to smile or cry." Or, "He was a jerk sometimes, and so damn full of himself, and I'd give anything to get to be annoyed with him again, you know?" And the other person would remember too and understand.

You would acknowledge he'd been kind of a shitty not-boyfriend, and we would talk that through too: the ways he hurt you. The mistakes you made. The closure you might never get from it. But that would help you move on, in a way. Eventually the missing-him would subside and he would become, for us both, a bittersweet memory. A tragic loss we shared.

I'm Team Lainie to the bitter end, but imagine if there were no teams to be chosen.

Dr. Rita thinks that's "something we can work on," the ability to allow myself to mourn Jackson without it feeling like it's a betrayal of you.

I'm not there yet.

I'm still working on admitting you hurt me.

You know what's strange? How completely fucking normal this week has been. You are on trial for Jackson's murder and I have been going to school like usual. Eating lunch with Dina Who I Usually Have Lunch With. Trading smiles with Ian in math class. (He hasn't tried to kiss me again—nor have I lunged at his face with mine— but we talk a little. Pass notes now and then. It's nice. Slow and nice. Way more normal than I thought it would be.) Doing homework. Having dinner with Peter and Adele. (They've been extra hawklike with the mood surveillance, but each day of your trial that I don't have a breakdown, they relax their feathers a touch.) Talking about my feelings with Dr. Rita. Reading about my best friend the murderer online for hours each night.

It's surreal.

In the sketch artist's drawings of the daily proceedings, you look pretty but steely. There's a harder look in your eyes than I can imagine actually being there, which I'm guessing means the artist thinks you're guilty. It's so weird that a courtroom sketch artist wouldn't try to be unbiased, but I watched an interview with one in a documentary about another case, and the artist talked about how at first he drew the defendant one way, but as the trial continued, he felt more sympathy toward the guy, and started drawing him differently. Isn't that wild? I guess the jury doesn't see the sketches until after they've given their verdict, but still. Everyone else does. And how you look definitely influences what people think, for better and for worse.

The coroner's testimony started today, and I swear, the press is practically salivating. People sharing stuff online are definitely drooling all over themselves. They're devouring every graphic detail.

I hadn't thought about this before, but I guess part of the reason people are so fascinated by Jackson's murder (besides that he was young, white, pretty, and rich, and you're young, white, and pretty), is they can't get over the idea of someone like you being violent. Girls and women aren't supposed to be killers. We're supposed to be nurturers, healers, and life-givers. I don't think anyone would be this obsessed if they thought Nitin smashed Jackson's head with a rock. But the idea of you doing it horrifies and thrills them.

Last night I looked up other murder cases where the alleged killer was female, and it's the same thing. People get obsessed. No one's surprised when men are violent. We expect it. Almost celebrate it. Men can kill for fun or out of entitlement or greed, and people only blink twice if the victims are famous or children, and white.

But an attractive female killer gets everyone all worked up. Uncomfortable. Excited. (Less so if it was self-defense. We expect that too: Women kill to escape men; men kill to own women. A lot more of the latter than the former, from what I can tell.) It's like society has this need for women and girls to be only victims. Your case fascinates because you defy the stereotypes. People want to find a way to explain it away and they can't. They reassure themselves you must be psycho.

Clicking around last night, I read a think piece you would love about how the world can't handle girls being bloody, unless the blood we shed is our own—once a month, or in childbirth, and keep that mess to yourself, please.

God, can you imagine if cis men cramped and bled every month? We would celebrate them with trophies and see it as a sign of their power. The jerkiest dudes would wear thin white pants and bleed through them on purpose, just to show off how tough they can be.

(Yes, I'm on the rag right now and bitter about it.)

I wonder if it's true that women are less violent. Maybe we're just smarter. I wonder how often women kill and don't get caught.

(I love that expression, though. *On the rag*. I love the dry, droll way you'd say it, like someone's chain-smoking grandma with four cats on your lap and no fucks left to give about anything.)

Anyway.

Blah blah blah.

I'm going to see if Adele will let me take one of her Ambiens. I'm sick of my brain and I want it to shut up and sleep.

Love,
Kayla

November 9
Channel 13 News

"Testimony continued today in this second week of the second-degree murder trial of teenager Elaine Baxter, who, as most of our viewers are aware by now, is accused of killing her summer-camp boyfriend, Jackson Winter, in August. Our reporter James Hsu is outside the Maplewash County Courthouse with updates. James, what can you tell us about what happened inside that courtroom today?"

"Thank you, Nina. Today jurors had another grueling day of hearing graphic testimony from local coroner Isabella O'Meara, who told the court on Friday about the blows Jackson Winter suffered to the head, which, she testified, in her opinion, were sustained before his body entered the water. Prosecutors entered into evidence last week several charts, photographs, and reports detailing the angles and extent of the two blows that the coroner's office ruled contributed significantly to Winter's subsequent death by drowning.

"In a lengthy cross-examination today, Baxter's lawyer, Michael Desir, seemingly tried to cast doubt on the coroner's level of expertise, asking a long string of questions about her medical experience before she became a county coroner, and how many cases of suspicious or violent death she has encountered in her years working as coroner in this sparsely populated rural area, which does not employ a full-time forensic pathologist or medical examiner. The answer boiled down to: not many.

"O'Meara remained cool on the witness stand and stayed firm in her testimony that in order for the blows to be self-inflicted, Winter would have had to, quote, 'dive in, hit the back of his head on a rock, then climb out and dive in to hit it again. Or, hit two perfectly positioned rocks, which investigators have not found to exist in that area of the lake,' end quote.

"Baxter's lawyer pressed, 'But he could have?' to which the coroner replied, 'That's extremely unlikely, but I suppose it could be technically possible under just the right circumstances, sure.'

"In redirect, the prosecutor sought to emphasize the unlikeliness of that possibility, asking, 'Is there any doubt in your mind that Jackson Winter received those two forceful blows to the head *before* his body entered the water?' to which the witness said simply, 'No.' 'Could there be doubt about that fact in anybody's mind?' the prosecutor pressed, and the witness replied, 'There shouldn't be.'

"It remains to be seen whether jurors found today's line of questioning from Baxter's defense attorney to seem credible, or merely desperate."

"Thank you, James."

"You're welcome, Nina."

November 9, 8:11 p.m.

hey

                                      hey

what are you up to

                               not much
                       homework and stuff

cool
listen,
I know we don't really talk abt what happened last summer or
what's going on with your friend
but I wanted to say
I'm here if you ever need someone
to listen or whatever

or to distract you from what's happening
if you don't want to talk about it
that's cool too
whatever you need, I'm here
just wanted to say that

I hope I didn't make things weird bringing it up
sorry if I did

no, it's fine

thanks

that means a lot

really

I'm good for now but I'll let you know if I need to talk

ok cool

see you at lunch?

yup, see you then

Camper and Counselor Interviews, Statements, and Posts
August 14–November 24

"The night of the big rainstorm, we were in the mess hall, playing charades in groups of ten. Jackson wasn't on our team at first, but he switched with someone so he could be with Lainie. Anyway. When his turn came, the phrase we had to guess was 'one brick at a time' and at first he was pantomiming the work of a bricklayer, but no one got it, so he made the 'sounds like' symbol for the second word, and started pointing to his crotch and miming like he was jerking off. Half the group was laughing too hard to guess and the rest of us were trying not to barf, and then time ran out and we didn't get it. Jackson threw his hands up and yelled 'Brick! Sounds like dick!' and shook his head like he was annoyed we were all so stupid. He was being a jerk. Lainie stood behind him and acted out picking up one of the invisible bricks he'd been building a wall with before, and hitting him over the head with it. Everyone cheered and she took a bow, and Jackson was grumpy like I thought maybe he might storm off, but he lifted her up and swung her around and she kicked and they both started laughing. It was Lainie's turn next and she had 'three peas in a pod' and Kayla guessed it right away and I forgot about the brick thing until now but it's weird, right? Like, a little too on point."

"The psycho-girlfriend-in-a-jealous-rage thing is like something from one of those movies my sister loves to watch. I always thought those plots were such bullshit. Like, does love really mess with people's heads so bad they decide they have to kill someone they can't have? I guess it happens, but I don't get it. Especially when you're our age. Just cry for a week and burn all their stuff, and move on and get over it. Don't *murder* them and ruin both your lives forever. I mean, yeesh. Who does that?"

"I'm still just really surprised. In the days before the murder, if that's what it was, Jackson and Lainie seemed extra lovey-dovey and good. No bickering or breakups and stuff like before. I'd heard they were actually planning to stay together after camp—that Jackson broke up with the girl from home or was going to, and they'd decided to give long-distance a shot. I was glad for them. They seemed in love.

"My friend heard that wasn't true, that they weren't planning on staying together, just making the most of the time they had left. But either way, it didn't seem like there was trouble. They seemed really happy and tight.

"I never in a million years would have believed something like this might happen to them."

"The last week of camp is so weird. This was my fourth year and it's always like that. Just ... weird. Extra intense. There's like this whole sense of doom hanging over everything because you're hyperaware every second that something you love is about to die.

"I mean, not *die* like that, but it's ending. Camp is ending, it's almost over, and it's sad. It's so sad. But also you're still there, there's still another week left, and you don't want to waste it being sad, but it hangs over everything. Everyone's a little grumpy and it sucks.

It sucks every year. There's nothing you can do about it. It's hard. Extra emotional.

"I think everyone's just really aware of the end coming, and some people react with this urgent extra closeness—like, desperate clinging—and others start to pull away before the end even gets there—like, preparing themselves—and there's all this hopelessness of knowing this world is about to end, we're all going our separate ways, and what we had can never be replicated. Even if you come back next year, it will be different. Different people, different dynamics. Still amazing, but different. It always ends. And whoever you were at camp kind of ends with it, because back home, no one will get it. The stories, the inside jokes. It's stuff only your camp friends can understand. And you still have them, but it's changed. You're not together anymore. It's sad. I really hate it.

"So, yeah. I wasn't paying that much attention to Lainie and Jackson or whoever because I had my own friends to say goodbye to while still trying not to make it seem like goodbye yet. Trying to squeeze the most out of my own last few days of summer. But it's a lot and I get how the emotions could make you snap. Every year, everyone cries on the last day, but some people really break down and get weird about it. Not weird like murderous, but weird like ... I don't know. I'm just rambling. I'll shut up about it now."

November 10

Dear Lainie,

Someone hacked the Camp Cavanick website last night and changed the logo to "A Summer of Fun. A Life Sentence for Murder. Exclusively for Teens!" The text below it promises "outdoor adventures, exciting challenges, confidence-building, friendship, and the chance to become fish food when your summer sweetheart loses her shit."

The main photo's been replaced with one of you, me, Nitin, and Jackson, sitting on the stone wall. Jackson looks at the camera smugly, like he just said something clever. You're laughing and leaning into me, caught mid-blink. My mouth's partway open and my hand's partway up, as though I'm making a counterargument. Nitin's side-eying Jackson like, *Dude, what the fuck.*

Jackson's uncle made a comment about the "sick mind" of the person responsible, but it's exactly the kind of thing Jackson would find hilarious. In fact, if he weren't dead, I'd be certain he's the one who did it. Jackson loved dark humor. It was one of the best things about him.

I keep thinking about something Jackson said, maybe two weeks before the end. We were alone by the wall, waiting for you to pee and get changed, and you were taking freaking forever. It was hot, and I was impatient, but Jackson seemed in a good mood. I said something about the wait and he shrugged. "Yeah, I'm used to waiting on Meghan."

"What would Meghan do if she knew about this?" I said. I lifted my chin toward our cabin.

Jackson smirked. "About what?"

I didn't smile.

He sighed. "She'd probably row here from Italy just to slap me. Or kill me," he said seriously. "As painfully yet efficiently as possible."

"That seems fair."

His smirk twisted into a grimace. "Actually, worse. She'd delete me from her phone and never acknowledge my existence again."

His shoulders slumped and he looked so bummed, I got worried and a little panicky. I shouldn't have asked about Meghan. I don't know what I'd been thinking.

This was bound to cause trouble in your relationship. Another breakup. More of his shit. This time partly my fault for reminding him of his guilt. You would be furious.

But you walked out of the cabin in your sunny-butt yellow shorts, Jackson brightened, and it was like the conversation never happened.

I was so relieved. The best thing for all of us was for the question of Meghan to go away. That's why I didn't tell you. I'm sorry.

But I can't stop wondering what she really would have done.

If Meghan didn't know then he was a lying, cheating asshole, she certainly knows now. But I don't know what she thinks about it. I can't tell.

I've watched videos of her entering the courthouse with his family, her expression grim, her posture perfect. I've studied photos of her at the funeral, dressed in black, wiping tears. I've zoomed in on her face, closer, closer, until her pupils fill the screen.

Would she really have been capable of murdering him? The pixels don't tell.

I've zoomed in on the rest of us too: you, me, Jackson, Nitin. Maddie, Rachel, Emma, Bree. Chef Beverly and Mika. A bunch of randos I don't even know. I've searched the face of every camper and counselor in every pic I can find from the summer. We look normal. Silly. Carefree. Alive. The pixels don't reveal what any of us are made of. The closer you get, the more the truth blurs.

Maybe a killer only looks like a killer in the moment just before, during, or after.

Maybe a liar, a good one, never shows it.

Maybe none of us know what we would or wouldn't do until the second it happens.

Whoa, Ian just texted. Dina told me he might, but I still didn't expect it.

Whoa whoa whoa.

Love,
Kayla

November 12

Dear Lainie,

I don't remember what your last fight with Jackson was about—the one before you kissed me the second time. It got hard to keep track. They were always over petty things, flaring up at almost random moments. But the fights themselves weren't petty at all. They hurt you.

You said it yourself: "That sticks-and-stones rhyme is utter bullshit."

The fights were never really over what they seemed to be over. Deep down, they were about you needing him, and him treating you like you were disposable. That's it. Every time. He hurt you so bad just by not really giving a shit, and you acted tough and doled it out as well as you took it when you were face-to-face with him in the moment, but as soon as we were alone afterward, you would crumple. His words were like an ice cream scoop digging out your chest—digging and digging, until the sides were scraped raw.

He hollowed you out, but the pain accumulated.

"He takes you for granted. That's not going to change. Aren't you tired of this?" I said that day for the millionth time.

You wiped tears and snot on the sleeve of your hoodie and nodded. "I know." But knowing never stopped you from hoping the next time might be different.

You chose the wrong person to trust with your heart. His not wanting you enough only made you want him more, and there was nothing I could do to shake you out of it. (Dr. Rita said Freud might have a thing or two to say about your desperation for Jackson's attention and your father's similar indifference. It made me hate her in the moment, but there's an appeal to thinking you couldn't help it.) It was so imbalanced.

It hollowed me out too, seeing you hurt like that. I felt useless and helpless and drained, time after time. Because what could I do? I could be angry for you, or sad with you. I could listen and commiserate and try to make you laugh. I could tell you again you deserved so much better, but I couldn't make you believe it—not deep down enough to convince you to truly walk away.

It hurt me to see you hurting, and it hurt even more to have you listen and agree, while knowing anything I said was just a bandage—one you would rip right off at the first chance to let him wound you again. It happened every time.

Except the last time. Somehow, the last time, my words got through. Maybe calling you out on the kiss had done it—woken you up to how messed up over him you'd become. Or maybe you were finally too exhausted to let things continue. I don't know. Whatever the cause, something shifted that day. I said the same words and you sniffled the same agreements, but it seemed to sink in.

"You're right," you said. "I'm done. For real this time. I promise." You squeezed my hand as though crushing my fingers would convince me. "We only have a week left, and we're going to make the most of it. You and me, together like before. Fuck Jackson. I've already wasted enough time on him. I don't need anyone here but you."

I braced myself for the backslide, but you meant it.

That first full day of being back to *us* was like coming up for air after swimming the full length of a pool underwater. We'd made it. We'd reached the other side and I could breathe again. I know you felt it too.

We were giddy with relief. Others were starting to get sad about the end approaching, but I was happier than I'd been in weeks. We had six days and nights left to pack as full as we could. And after that we would text, visit, and write. We'd already promised. I wasn't sad that camp was ending in less than a week. I was elated you and Jackson had ended first.

You were back. *We* were back. Nothing could come between us. Remember?

The next days were the best days. I thought we'd weathered the storm and come out closer and stronger. I had no idea we were smack in the eye of the hurricane. Did you?

I don't think so. You're a good actress, but not that good. I've always been able to read how you're feeling. When the winds picked back up and blew you off your feet, I saw it in your face right away. After two and a half blissfully Jackson-free days, he'd returned. I knew it before you spoke. Your eyes had that floaty, faraway, dazed-but-fine-with-it look. Your lips twitched with the secret.

"Oh no," I said as you approached. "No. Tell me you didn't—don't do this. Don't take him back again. Please."

You slid in across from me at the picnic table by the lake and shook your head, but your smile still held the news I dreaded. "It's not what you think," you said.

It was exactly what I thought.

"I didn't take him back. I've been ignoring him for days, just like I promised. And I've felt great. He came up to me this morning and I totally shrugged him off. He tried telling me he misses me and I said, 'Too bad for you. And too bad you didn't appreciate me when I was willing to be around. I'm over it. Your loss.' And I turned and walked away."

I waited. I knew there was more.

"So when he came to find me again and was like, 'Can we talk?' I was like, 'Whatever,' because there's nothing he can say that would make me go back to that, you know? He has a girlfriend. I'm just some *challenge* for him—like, a mountain he wants to climb, just to prove he can—and not even one he takes seriously. But he can't reach the top because I'll always be too much mountain for him, and it makes him want to tear me down, like you said. I know that now. I get it."

"Uh-huh." A thousand sirens were going off in my head. Couldn't you hear them?

"But . . . Kayla . . . he gets it too. He really does." I kept my mouth shut. You couldn't even make eye contact. "He wants us to try again, and he promises, *promises* things will be different. He broke up with Meghan because he realized he loves me. He wants us to be together for real."

You looked at me then, and the hope in your face broke me open. You wanted me to be happy for you. You wanted me to believe.

"He begged. Like, down on his knees. Begged and apologized for everything he's put me through. It sounds corny, but it was actually really sweet," you said. "You'll see. He's changed."

I wanted to point out those theatrics sounded exactly like more of the same. He'd even made his *apology* all about him. A spectacle.

But you'd already made up your mind. Even if I said the words out loud, you wouldn't hear them. So I didn't.

The fifth rule of crime is: Always Stick Together. Where you went, I went. So I followed you back down the rabbit hole.

Here we are: Off with your head.

Love,
Kayla

November 13

Dear Lainie,

It's Friday the 13th and I'm thinking of you, because who else claims thirteen as their lucky number?

I feel like that says so much about you, though I don't know exactly what. That you're completely unsuperstitious, for one. (Ugh, that's apparently not a real word, but those red dots won't stop me. SUCK IT, SPELL-CHECK. Haha, maybe I'm a rebel after all.) That you like to push your luck, for another. (Is it still pushing your luck if you aren't superstitious? I'm going with yes, so shush.) That you're cooler and more badass than any fool with a regular old lucky number, for sure.

I don't know why primes are inherently cooler than other numbers, but they are—which is strange, since they're mostly so odd.

Ba-dum-ching! (Sorry. Sorry! Please stop groaning. Sorry.)

My lucky number is eight. Le sigh. Without you, I'm not all that interesting.

In English today, Ms. Pan had two words up on the board that looked like random-letter barf, but were not: triskaidekaphobia and paraskevidekatriaphobia. Triskaidekaphobia is a fear of the number thirteen. Paraskevidekatriaphobia is a fear of Friday the 13th (the day, not the movie). They come from the Greek words for *thirteen*, *fear*, and *Friday*. I will never remember how to spell or pronounce them, but I love that they exist.

When I told Dina, they immediately began calculating how

many Scrabble points each word would be worth if it could fit on a Scrabble board, which it could not. Dina is possibly even more random than I am. I wonder sometimes what you would think of them.

If it weren't your favorite number—if you had a hint of triskaidekaphobia—maybe you would have thought twice when I said, "Well . . . thirteenth time's the charm, right?" at the news of you and Jackson getting back together. Instead, you hugged me and beamed, and felt lucky, I guess.

Things really did seem different with him the last week, though, I admit it. He seemed sweeter. More attentive and appreciative. Much closer to the kind of boyfriend I thought you deserved. I was glad to see you happy. But it was hard for me too.

With Jackson no longer being such a shithead, you needed me less, and abandoned me a lot more often. I'm not blaming you—please don't think that. I know you didn't leave me out on purpose, and I get why you needed time alone with him. It's not like I wanted to hang around while you guys made out or whatever. But it still felt lonely.

Even when we did hang just you and me, your attention was often elsewhere. That stank. But what could I say? Don't spend time with your boyfriend? I wish you'd break up again even though you're happy? It's not fair that he's being good to you now? Your top priority has to be me? No way. Expressing any of that would be ridiculous and kind of psycho.

It was a problem with no good solution, so I tried to just let it be. To not mind sharing you. To trust we were good and you loved me. To assure myself you weren't really slipping away. To stop measuring the sides of our awkward, uneven triangle.

The fact that Nitin had stopped hanging out with us made the problem much worse. If he'd still been around, it would have been a group thing, instead of Jackson intruding on you-and-me time, or me intruding on you and Jackson. I don't know if he got sick of Jackson or all of us or what, but he was barely around and he never snuck out anymore. I asked Jackson point-blank what he had done to push Nitin away, but Jackson scrunched up his face and said, "Huh?" and I dropped it. It definitely struck me as weird, though.

Maybe I should have tried hanging with other people too, but we only had a few days left. I didn't want new friends, or to forfeit my time left with you. It was third wheel or nothing, so I went with third wheel.

It was fine, mostly. The three of us fell into a rhythm that worked pretty well. I stopped saying "Ew" when he kissed you in front of me (you're welcome) and he didn't pout when we cracked each other up over something he wasn't in on or didn't get. I'd have preferred getting you all to myself, and so would he, but we each respected why the other was important to you, and tried to make the best of it. A truce, for your sake.

I'm sure you knew I was still cautious and skeptical. I tried to hide it, but it was there, just like our apparent agreement not to speak of it. We barely talked about Jackson at all that week, or about how things were going with him. It was the first time any topic felt off-limits between us, and I felt the distance it caused—a distance of things unsaid. But I held my tongue because I loved you, and you'd asked me to give him another chance—one he seemed to be living up to. If you could forgive him, I would forgive him. I was almost there. You had to know I was trying.

If we'd had the whole week to pretend things were normal, I think by now they truly would be. I mean, if it hadn't all been an enormous lie.

Was it lucky or unlucky how the truth came to light? That day was the thirteenth too. A Thursday—what should have been two days before the end of the best summer of my life. (Has it really been only three months since it happened? It feels like a whole other lifetime. I guess in some ways, it was.)

I had you to myself that morning, and the plan was to go canoeing. Sunscreen applied, life vests on, paddles in hand, boat signed out and ready. I was in a good mood and you were grumpy-ish, but I figured that would improve once we got out on the water. You slapped the back of your neck and said, "Ugh, I forgot bug spray. They're eating me alive."

"So go get it."

You heaved a dramatic sigh. "I'm too lazy," you said, and I realized you might stay cranky after all.

I set my paddle down. "I'll get you some."

You brightened. "Really?"

"Sure. I want to grab my sunglasses anyway." And I didn't want mosquitoes shortening our trip.

"You're the best."

I ran to the cabin and returned with the OFF!. I was too late. An enormous, face-sucking pest had found you.

I pretended to smack him. "Got one!" I said. You pulled yourself off him and laughed. I aimed the nozzle at Jackson's face. "Shoot, he's still moving. You might need extra-strength stuff to get rid of this one."

Jackson ducked and covered his eyes, and you took the container. I wouldn't have sprayed it, you know. Blinding him was not in my best interest. I just wanted us to get in the canoe. "I thought you were in the computer lab," I said.

He shrugged. "Yeah, but I'm waiting on the 3D printer. Figured I would sneak out here and see if I could find my girl. You need help tipping over the canoe?"

"No," I said. What was with Jackson and his obsession about entering the lake in dangerous ways? "We're not tipping." *And you're not going with us*, I added silently. I raised my eyebrows at you and you frowned slightly. Were you really about to invite him to come along?

You didn't have to. Nitin showed up out of nowhere and asked, "Hey, do you guys need a fourth?" I'd never been so happy to see him.

We both smiled and said "Perfect" at the same time. I meant, *Perfect, you can go with Jackson*, but you said, "You go with Kayla, and Jackson will go with me."

I should have spoken up. I should have told Jackson to shove off. But I didn't. I watched you lift one end of the canoe, *our* canoe, and carry it to the water. Watched him steady it while you climbed in front. Returned your wave as he used his paddle to push off from the rocks.

Nitin returned with a life vest and said, "Ready?" I nodded, and that was it. We carried our boat to the water. No more chance to avoid what happened next.

I assumed we at least would stick together—that you would wait so we could paddle our boat beside yours—but by the time we'd launched, you were already well across the lake. "You okay with going this way?" Nitin asked as he steered us west along the shore. That kept the sun on our backs and meant we occasionally would get some shade. It was the smart choice. I glanced over at you and Jackson to signal you, but you weren't even looking my way.

"Whatever you want," I told Nitin. "I'm easy."

I heard the low rumble of Jackson's voice, the high squeal of your laughter. I dug my paddle into the water and tried to sweep away the whole damn lake. We paddled in silence for a while.

"I don't like it either," Nitin said.

"What?" I asked.

"Seeing them back together."

I was too surprised to respond. He continued. "He's such a dick sometimes. It's hard to watch. She deserves better."

On principle, I agreed, yet I felt the need to defend you. "She knows what she's doing," I said. "It's her choice to make, not ours." (Dr. Rita has said a few times, "You're very loyal." It's more of an observation than a compliment when she says it, but each time I agree and say thank you. It's true, I am loyal. And I want to be.)

"Yeah, of course," Nitin said. "I just hate seeing her sign up to get hurt."

"Isn't he your friend?" I said. Though lately they'd been far from tight.

I turned in time to see him shrug. "As much as he is yours, I guess."

Fair point.

They were definitely an odd pairing—Nitin so thoughtful, and Jackson so . . . not. But Nitin was basically a social chameleon—he could fit in anywhere, with anyone, and seemed welcome in every group. But maybe that didn't mean he liked everyone.

I faced forward again. We'd stopped paddling and the canoe was drifting, but that was fine. I couldn't paddle and focus on whatever was happening in this strange conversation. It felt like Nitin had maybe sought me out to tell me something specific, but I wasn't sure what or if I wanted to hear it.

"Yeah, well. She seems happy this time. And he's really all-in," I said.

Nitin snorted. I spun around. I did not like him judging you like that. What business of his was any of it?

"*What.* You're not around to see, but it's different now. They're much better since he broke up with his girlfriend. No more bickering and he's really sweet to her. I'm glad for them," I said, convincing myself too as the words came out.

I was laying it on thick, but his acting like he knew anything about you or what was best for you was honestly pissing me off. I'd never noticed he could be so annoying.

Nitin paused. "Is that what he told her? He broke up with his girlfriend?" he said.

"Yes," I snapped. "Last weekend." I lifted the paddle off my lap and dipped it in again. "As you can imagine, that changes a lot." My tone was clear: end of discussion.

Nitin cleared his throat. "Kayla."

I whipped around, ready to explode. His sad expression snuffed the fuse, and my stomach sank.

"He didn't break up with Meghan," he said carefully. I stared. "Not from the way he was talking about her in the cabin last night."

Nitin reddened and looked away. "He's not . . . He's not a great person, really."

The boat rocked in the waves of a speed boat that flew past. I wanted to vomit.

He'd been feeding you lies and you'd swallowed them. You'd gobbled them up and asked for more.

"Are you sure?" I asked quietly.

He nodded. "I'm sorry."

I shook my head and swiveled to face forward. The sun glistened off the water and the breeze was still perfect, but it felt like the world had been shot to hell. Tears stung my eyes. The news wasn't merely a gut punch. It seemed to reach down my throat and twist my guts right out. And if learning of Jackson's betrayal affected *me* so badly, how was it going to affect you?

I sat in shock for a long moment. At some point Nitin had started paddling, but we must have been moving again for a while before I noticed. I gripped my paddle, readied the blade, and sliced it through the water.

We went all the way down to the boundary signs ("Ahoy, Camp Cavanick campers! Turn your vessels here") and all the way back in silence. My arms ached. When we returned to shore, you and

Jackson were nowhere in sight, but your canoe was back on the rack. My heart ached too.

We hung our life vests and stacked our paddles, and Nitin gave me an apologetic grimace. "You're a good friend," he said.

"Thanks," I answered, not knowing if he meant to him or to you or in general or what. And what was I supposed to do with that? Did Nitin want me to tell you the truth that would hurt you? Was that the "good friend" thing to do? Or did he mean it was good of me to protect and defend you, even if that meant swallowing Jackson's poison to spare you? It felt corrosive in my veins already. I didn't want to share that feeling with you.

And yet. We'd never lied to each other. Friends owe friends the truth.

Hadn't I just snapped at Nitin for basically second-guessing your right to decide for yourself? You didn't need me to filter your reality. Wouldn't holding this in cause more harm?

I don't know. I don't know what was right, or what could have been. If I hadn't told you what Nitin said, might Jackson still be alive?

Stop. Don't answer that.

Don't.

Love,
Kayla

November 13
Channel 5 News

"There was a somber mood in the courthouse today as jurors heard testimony from two prosecution witnesses about the blue size-medium hooded sweatshirt allegedly belonging to Elaine Baxter, which was found under the steps to Sweetwater Cabin—the cabin Miss Baxter and fifteen other campers shared last summer—and which the state says was stained with Jackson Winter's blood.

"Camp director Skip Pluta testified he recovered the hoodie from behind the two wooden steps to the girls' cabin several days after the abrupt end to the camp session, where, he said, it appeared to have been stashed deliberately by someone attempting to hide it—perhaps intending to retrieve and destroy it later, or perhaps hoping it might stay there and never be found. When Pluta recognized the hoodie as potentially belonging to Miss Baxter—he recalled she wore an identical garment throughout the summer, and prosecutors submitted into evidence multiple official camp photos, which Pluta identified as being of Miss Baxter in what appears to be the hoodie in question—he immediately called the police, even before noticing several dark stains on its sleeves.

"Next, forensic scientist Kacey Proffert took the stand and walked the court through her analysis of several DNA samples taken from the hoodie—the bloodstains on which, she determined, are a clear match to Jackson Winter's DNA. Proffert said the sweatshirt contained non-blood DNA samples from at least three other people, including Elaine Baxter, but that most of the DNA 'by far' was identifiable as belonging to either the victim or the defendant.

"The forensic expert testified she did not believe the presence of non-blood DNA from at least two other individuals to be unusual or suspicious, given the communal living situation in which the garment had been worn throughout the summer, where it easily would have come in contact with many other people, and been sent to the laundry at most once per week.

"In cross-examination, Baxter's lawyer focused less on the DNA evidence and more on other, seemingly unrelated questions, such as grilling the camp director about the lack of bed checks at Camp Cavanick, and whether every other camper and counselor's whereabouts on the night of the alleged murder could be accounted for.

"'Can you tell me with certainty that there were no trespassers on the property the night of Jackson Winter's death?' the lawyer asked. 'I cannot,' the director replied, and the lawyer left it at that.

"The prosecutor is expected to call her final witnesses in the opening days of next week, after which we will finally hear the details of Elaine Baxter's defense.

"Reporting live from Maplewash County Courthouse in Jaspertown, I'm Kay Douglass, Channel Five News."

November 13, 9:52 p.m.

hey

can I ask you something?

Hi

Sure, of course

why were you avoiding us?

?

at the end

I mean

the last week or two of camp

you stopped hanging with L&J and me

I just felt like you were avoiding us or something

were you?

I'm sorry

I wasn't avoiding you

I don't know, I just freaked out I guess

about what?

About nothing. everything. I don't know

It got weird

Don't you think?

                                                    well, obviously

But before that

I mean

before he died

it seemed less fun

uncomfortable sometimes

I don't know

I guess I just got sick of them and it was easier with other people

or something

I'm sorry

it wasn't you

I didn't think you would notice, to be honest

                                                         oh

                                                         ok

you were pretty wrapped up in Lainie and her shit

                                                her shit???

Sorry
She and Jackson were a little much sometimes
mostly Jackson
But her too

It brought flashbacks of my uncle when he would visit
Jackson did
He was not a great guy
my uncle I mean

I shouldn't compare them

I just needed to pull back
and I was becoming better friends with some other guys from our
cabin so
I guess I switched to mostly hanging with them instead

I wonder all the time if I hadn't if that would have changed things

                                        I don't think so

                                but I know what you mean
                                survivor's guilt or whatever

Yeah

I shouldn't have told you

about Meghan and him

it's not your fault

Thanks for saying that

I mean it

thanks
It's good to hear from you

yeah
take care

You too

November 13, 11:23 p.m.

can I ask you something else?

Okay

were you in love with her?

um
Weren't we all, a little bit?

touché

I think no
not exactly
but I did wish I could protect her sometimes
from anything bad
If she needed that
More like brotherly love I guess

I didn't do anything though

I believe you
but I believed her too

You don't anymore?

I don't know

I don't know what to believe

I'm sorry

November 15

Dear Lainie,

Dr. Rita and I had a special bonus session yesterday to prepare me for seeing you again. It helped me think through what I might want to say, though I don't think I'll really know how tomorrow should go until I get there. Until I'm with you.

I'm nervous. It's going to be weird in so many ways, making the drive back to camp (almost) but with the air cold and the leaves dead and gone, and everything different. It will be weird seeing you in a courtroom instead of a cabin, and with a bunch of adults who aren't counselors around. It's weird we won't escape to the dock and won't even get to talk, really. I won't see any stars or the moon while I'm there. I'll have to answer terrible questions.

My parents say there's nothing for me to be nervous about. They told me to just answer the questions as best I can, and not worry about trying to protect you. That's not my job, they say, even if I am your best friend—it's your lawyer's. And it's not my job to decide what's true—it's the jury's. My only job is to share what I know and be as honest and thorough as possible.

It's funny how easy that sounds when they say it.

I'll try. I remember the sixth rule of crime: Keep It Simple. The more straightforward the plan, the fewer ways to fuck it up. (Jackson never fully grasped that. He always wanted us to go paddleboarding at night, or raid the kitchen, or really hitchhike into town. But you were the midnight mastermind, not him. If he wanted to fool around and get caught pulling off an elaborate scheme for the thrill of it, he was on his own. The simplicity of our nighttime escapes was part of the beauty of them.)

But "just tell the truth" isn't as simple as people want it to be. Some truths are misleading. Some sit side by side with true lies. And many are subjective. That's why this whole thing is so tough to untangle. (That and the fact that it's a big fucking mess, and I'm a big fucking mess when I think about it. Ugh.)

There are things I know for sure are untrue, but that doesn't stop them from feeling true. And vice versa: there are true, real things about what happened this summer that just seem wrong when I look at them. It's like those "Which line is longer?" illusions where even once you know the two lines are the same length, you can't help but see one as shorter. You're supposed to see one as shorter. The illusion was designed that way.

How many of your deceptions were designed to mislead, and which ones fooled even you? How many did you want to believe? Does that matter?

Let's be clear: You weren't the only liar around. Can you be blamed for the ways you let Jackson deceive you? Can you be blamed for telling me lies you desperately wanted us both to swallow? Does it matter if we should have known better? Does it matter if, deep down, you did? Does that change how people should judge what happened when the truth was forced to light? Or how *I* should judge it?

Maybe. I don't know.

Dr. Rita said, "What if I said to you, 'You know what? We'll never know. You will never learn what was really in her heart and mind—or his—or what happened that night. You just won't.' How does that feel? Does it change anything for you? Or maybe help you let go of some of this pressure to figure it all out and get it right?"

I stared at the carpet and watched the pattern blur to mush, then separate out into focus. I shrugged. "Not really. The jury will still decide, based in part on what I tell them. So it matters if I have things right or wrong, even if I only know a piece of it."

She waited for me to continue. That's one of her techniques. Dr. Rita is extremely comfortable sitting in silence for long stretches of time. The thing is, I am too. But there was something I'd been wanting to bring up.

"Do you think it's possible Jackson might have been a psychopath?" I asked.

She shifted in her chair but kept her face steady. She never laughs at my randomness like you did. "What makes you wonder that?"

"I don't know. I've been reading about them online," I said.

"Psychopaths?"

"Yeah. Some people are saying Lainie could be one."

She didn't react. I'm guessing the idea wasn't news to her. She probably goes online too.

I explained anyway. "Because of the lying. And her charisma—psychopaths are charming. And they're impulsive and manipulative and irresponsible. And, like, promiscuous."

I blushed when I said that last part. I don't think of you that way, for the record. But other people do. Other people suck. I hate that double standard. "And I guess because of the shoplifting and stuff.

Because that's juvenile delinquent behavior."

Dr. Rita nodded. "And Jackson?"

"Well, I was looking at the list of signs—like, how you know if someone's a psychopath—and I thought, yeah, you can twist these to make them apply to her, but some things on the list apply to Jackson too. He was definitely manipulative and thrill-seeking, and charming in his own way. Not to mention entitled—he had a super-inflated sense of self, and lacked empathy, from the way he treated her. And he was far more promiscuous than she was, I'd say, since he was the one who was cheating. He was irresponsible and unremorseful. Those are psychopathic traits, right?"

"They can be," Dr. Rita said carefully.

"So why are people saying that about her and not him?" I stopped myself. Even I knew that sounded ridiculous. He's dead. You're not. I exhaled.

"Do you think she is?" I asked the carpet.

"It would be unethical of me to even try to diagnose someone who is not under my care and observation," Dr. Rita said. "Jackson *or* Lainie. And like most disorders, psychopathy isn't a straight either-or that conforms to a neat checklist. It exists on a continuum. There's a spectrum of psychopathic behavior and ways it can be exhibited."

I was sick of this topic. I diverted. "Okay, so how about me? Could I be a psychopath?"

She smiled. "You are not."

"You don't think I'm charming enough to be that manipulative?" I said, half joking.

"I think you feel things very deeply," she said, "and that this whole thing has you understandably confused and very hurt."

I looked away and stopped breathing.

"You have a strong sense of loyalty and an innate pull toward justice, and you're very protective of the friends you love. It's deeply hurtful for you to think that your loyalty and trust may have been abused or misplaced," she said. She wasn't wrong, but it made my chest burn to hear it.

"You experienced something extremely traumatic and horrible, and you're processing it the best you can. I know it's hard. I think you're doing an amazing job, moving on from something that sad and painful. I think these two losses will always be sad for you, but the pain will get better. And I know whatever happens in that courtroom this week, you'll be okay. It will be okay."

I burst into tears. Is that weird? She let me cry, and nudged the tissue box closer. Then our session was over.

Remember that walk we took in the summer rain, the day it poured and poured, and everyone grumbled and grouched and tried to avoid having to go outside? You got bored and said, "Let's go," so I followed, and we were instantly drenched—our clothes soaked, our hair plastered, our sandals squishing and sloshing—and for a second it was weird, but I got used to it. The water gushed over my face and ran into my ears while we walked on the path by the lake, which was pebbled by raindrops and green-gray like slate. The rain was warm and I felt free and brave and alive, being in it, and with everyone else stuck inside playing card games or whatever, it was like the whole outdoors was ours alone.

When we returned, we dripped massive puddles on the floor, and my fingers were all puckered and wrinkled, and we took hot showers, long ones, even though we'd basically just showered in the rain. But getting out of the shower after the rain walk, how cleaner than clean that felt? Like we'd been rinsed completely, cleansed inside and out? This cry and release felt like that. Like I've been holding on and holding on and holding on tight, and I finally just let go.

See you tomorrow.

Love,
Kayla

P.S. Lainie, if I'm wrong about this—about you—just give me a sign. I'll change the whole story. I'll say what needs to be said. I will lengthen the shadow of doubt, somehow.

None of this is "reasonable."

Just come back to me.

Please.

November 16

Maplewash County Courthouse

ATTORNEY DAVIS: State will call Kayla Martin to the stand.

THE CLERK: Please raise your right hand. Do you swear that you will tell the truth, the whole truth, and nothing but the truth, so help you God?

THE WITNESS: I do.

THE CLERK: Please be seated. Please state your name and spell your last name for the record.

THE WITNESS: Kayla Martin, M-A-R-T-I-N.

ATTORNEY DAVIS: Hi, Kayla. How old are you?

THE WITNESS: I'm sixteen.

ATTORNEY DAVIS: And what is your relationship to the defendant, Elaine Baxter?

THE WITNESS: She's my best friend.

ATTORNEY DAVIS: Could you please describe how you met the defendant, and when you two became friends?

THE WITNESS: I met her last summer at Camp Cavanick. We were in the same cabin and Lainie had the top bunk above mine, so I guess we met on the first day. We became friends pretty quickly. We hung out the first time the third night, and we were together every day after that.

ATTORNEY DAVIS: And what kinds of things did you do together?

THE WITNESS: Um. Camp things? Like, activities and stuff. But mostly we talked.

ATTORNEY DAVIS: What did you talk about?

THE WITNESS: Everything.

ATTORNEY DAVIS: Did you talk about Jackson Winter?

THE WITNESS: Sometimes. After we met him, yeah.

ATTORNEY DAVIS: These conversations you would have with Miss Baxter, did they happen during the daytime?

THE WITNESS: Yes.

ATTORNEY DAVIS: And at night?

THE WITNESS: Yes.

ATTORNEY DAVIS: How about after lights-out?

THE WITNESS: Sometimes, yes.

ATTORNEY DAVIS: Where did you talk after lights-out?

THE WITNESS: Uh, outside. Like, out on the dock.

ATTORNEY DAVIS: On the dock at the lake?

THE WITNESS: Yes.

ATTORNEY DAVIS: How did you get there after lights-out?

THE WITNESS: We snuck out.

ATTORNEY DAVIS: You and Miss Baxter?

THE WITNESS: Yes.

ATTORNEY DAVIS: And when you snuck out after hours to go down to the lake, were you and Miss Baxter aware you were breaking camp rules?

THE WITNESS: Yes.

ATTORNEY DAVIS: Whose idea was it to sneak out and break the rules like that?

THE WITNESS: Uh, Lainie's, I guess.

ATTORNEY DAVIS: Miss Baxter was the instigator?

THE WITNESS: Yes. But I went along with it. I liked sneaking out too. It was harmless. And fun.

ATTORNEY DAVIS: Okay. When you snuck out at night, was it just the two of you doing it?

THE WITNESS: At first.

ATTORNEY DAVIS: But not always?

THE WITNESS: No. Sometimes Jackson and a friend would join us. Or just Jackson.

ATTORNEY DAVIS: I see. And did the three of you—you, Lainie, and Jackson—did you spend a lot of time together?

THE WITNESS: Yes.

ATTORNEY DAVIS: And as Elaine Baxter's best friend, someone who spent a lot of time with her and Jackson Winter together, how would you characterize their relationship?

THE WITNESS: Um. They were, uh . . . friends? And sometimes more than that?

ATTORNEY DAVIS: More than friends?

THE WITNESS: Yeah. They were together, on and off.

ATTORNEY DAVIS: Together how?

THE WITNESS: Um, like a couple.

ATTORNEY DAVIS: They were a couple?

THE WITNESS: Yes and no.

ATTORNEY DAVIS: You'll have to explain that a little more, please, so the jury and I can understand it. Was Miss Baxter Jackson Winter's girlfriend?

THE WITNESS: No.

ATTORNEY DAVIS: But they did things that couples do?

THE WITNESS: I guess. Sometimes.

ATTORNEY DAVIS: Like what?

THE WITNESS: Um. Kissing. Holding hands. Uh, stuff like that.

ATTORNEY DAVIS: But the, uh, kissing and, um, other things that they did, that didn't make her his girlfriend?

THE WITNESS: No.

ATTORNEY DAVIS: Huh. Why not?

THE WITNESS: He, uh—he had a different girlfriend. Not at camp. He had a girlfriend back home.

ATTORNEY DAVIS: Did Miss Baxter know about Jackson's real girlfriend?

THE WITNESS: Yes, she did.

ATTORNEY DAVIS: Did she ever tell you how she felt about that?

THE WITNESS: Yes.

ATTORNEY DAVIS: When she talked about Jackson having a girlfriend who wasn't her, what did she say?

THE WITNESS: Different stuff. She was fine with it sometimes. Other times it made her feel angry or sad.

ATTORNEY DAVIS: Jealous?

THE WITNESS: Sure.

ATTORNEY DAVIS: Was it something they fought about?

THE WITNESS: Yes.

ATTORNEY DAVIS: How often did you witness them fighting, about that or other things?

THE WITNESS: I don't— It's hard to say. They bickered a lot. Sometimes kidding, sometimes not. Jackson seemed to enjoy it, kind of egging her on. I guess it got serious every week or so. They'd break up, get back together, break up again. I lost track. It's just how they were together.

ATTORNEY DAVIS: Did these fights and breakups take a toll on Miss Baxter emotionally, would you say?

THE WITNESS: I'm not sure what you mean.

ATTORNEY DAVIS: Did they upset her?

THE WITNESS: Yes.

ATTORNEY DAVIS: Kayla, did you ever hear Elaine Baxter talk about killing Jackson Winter?

THE WITNESS: Uh . . .

ATTORNEY DAVIS: Yes or no, please.

THE WITNESS: Yes, but it was joking.

ATTORNEY DAVIS: She would joke about killing him?

THE WITNESS: Yes.

ATTORNEY DAVIS: How often?

THE WITNESS: I don't know. Now and then.

ATTORNEY DAVIS: You heard her joke about killing him more than once?

THE WITNESS: Yes.

ATTORNEY DAVIS: More than three times?

THE WITNESS: Yes.

ATTORNEY DAVIS: More than, say, a dozen times?

THE WITNESS: I guess so. Probably, yes. It was, like, an ongoing thing.

ATTORNEY DAVIS: I see. And when Elaine Baxter would talk about killing Jackson Winter, did she ever sound upset with him?

THE WITNESS: She'd— I mean, not usually. It was usually something they joked about together. Not a real thing. Not angry. Just something silly. An inside joke.

ATTORNEY DAVIS: You said "usually." But not always? She sometimes said it to you when she was upset?

THE WITNESS: [unintelligible]

JUDGE RODRIGUEZ: Could the witness please repeat that into the microphone?

THE WITNESS: Yes. I mean, I guess so.

ATTORNEY DAVIS: Did you hear Miss Baxter talk about killing Jackson in the days before he died?

THE WITNESS: Yes, but—

ATTORNEY DAVIS: Did you see her get upset about Jackson having another girlfriend in the days before he died?

THE WITNESS: I— It's not like that. It was complicated.

ATTORNEY DAVIS: Complicated how?

THE WITNESS: They'd broken up. Him and his girlfriend. Or Lainie thought so. She told me— She told me he wanted to be with her for real, and he had broken up with his girlfriend, and they were going to stay together. She was happy. Those last several days, they were happy. Things were better.

ATTORNEY DAVIS: And was it true? Had Jackson broken up with his girlfriend?

THE WITNESS: No.

ATTORNEY DAVIS: How do you know that?

THE WITNESS: Someone told me. A guy in his cabin. He said Jackson and Meghan were still together, that the breakup was a lie.

ATTORNEY DAVIS: What day did you learn this?

THE WITNESS: The, uh— Thursday morning. The thirteenth.

ATTORNEY DAVIS: Thursday the thirteenth. Meaning, the morning before Jackson died? The last morning he was alive?

THE WITNESS: Yes.

ATTORNEY DAVIS: And what did you do with this news when you heard it?

THE WITNESS: I told Lainie. Not right away. She was with him. But later that night, when I got her alone, I told her.

ATTORNEY DAVIS: What time was it when you told her, do you remember that?

THE WITNESS: After dinner. It was getting dark. So, uh, sometime around eight or nine p.m., I guess.

ATTORNEY DAVIS: How did Miss Baxter react when you told her?

THE WITNESS: She was upset. She didn't want to believe it.

ATTORNEY DAVIS: But she did believe it?

THE WITNESS: I don't know. She didn't say.

ATTORNEY DAVIS: Did she get angry?

THE WITNESS: Not really. She was pretty calm. I think she was kind of tired of the whole thing, and waiting to react until she could ask him about it.

ATTORNEY DAVIS: She planned to ask him if it was true? To confront him?

THE WITNESS: I'm not sure. I assumed so.

ATTORNEY DAVIS: But you didn't see it?

THE WITNESS: No. He came over to us and they were being normal, kind of cuddly, and there were a lot of people around at the campfire. It wasn't a good or private time for them to talk.

ATTORNEY DAVIS: Do you know if they found a private time to talk later?

THE WITNESS: Um. I think so. I don't know for sure, I guess.

ATTORNEY DAVIS: You didn't see them talking alone that night before he died?

THE WITNESS: No, I didn't see it.

ATTORNEY DAVIS: So on what basis would you assume they did?

THE WITNESS: They— I saw her leave the cabin. That night. She snuck out to go meet him.

ATTORNEY DAVIS: You saw Elaine Baxter leave the cabin in the middle of the night on Thursday, August thirteenth?

THE WITNESS: Yes.

ATTORNEY DAVIS: What time was this, approximately?

THE WITNESS: After midnight, I think. We always snuck out after midnight. So I guess it was technically the fourteenth.

ATTORNEY DAVIS: But you didn't sneak out with her that night?

THE WITNESS: No.

ATTORNEY DAVIS: Why not?

THE WITNESS: I wasn't— She didn't invite me. I knew they wanted to meet up alone.

ATTORNEY DAVIS: She and Jackson Winter?

THE WITNESS: Yes.

ATTORNEY DAVIS: And when she left the cabin after midnight in the early hours of August fourteenth, how do you know where she went?

THE WITNESS: Because we always went to the dock. And she was dressed for it. She had her hoodie on, because it got chilly sometimes on the lake, and she was barefoot but picked up her shoes to slip on. We put our shoes on outside to make less noise inside the cabin.

ATTORNEY DAVIS: So you saw Miss Baxter leave the cabin after midnight, wearing a hoodie and carrying shoes. Did you see her come back in?

THE WITNESS: Yes.

ATTORNEY DAVIS: What time was it when she came back?

THE WITNESS: I don't know.

ATTORNEY DAVIS: Soon after she left?

THE WITNESS: No.

ATTORNEY DAVIS: How do you know that?

THE WITNESS: Because . . . because I fell back asleep, and kind of woke up a while later and looked to see what time it was. It was 2:13. I thought she must already have come back and I must have slept through it, and I went to sleep again. But when she came back for real, I woke up and saw her, so I know it was after that, but I don't know how long I'd been asleep. It could have been minutes or hours. I didn't look at a clock that time.

ATTORNEY DAVIS: Was it still dark?

THE WITNESS: It was still dark.

ATTORNEY DAVIS: But you could see clearly that the person who returned was Miss Baxter?

THE WITNESS: I know the way she moves and I could feel her climb up to her bunk. It kind of shakes the bed a little when she puts her weight on it.

ATTORNEY DAVIS: When she returned to the cabin, sometime after 2:13 a.m., was she still wearing the same hooded sweatshirt?

THE WITNESS: I don't know.

ATTORNEY DAVIS: You don't know?

THE WITNESS: I don't remember. I didn't notice. And there wasn't as much moonlight then.

ATTORNEY DAVIS: In the morning, did she have that hoodie on?

THE WITNESS: No.

ATTORNEY DAVIS: Did you ever see her wearing the hoodie again, or see the hoodie again without her wearing it?

THE WITNESS: No. I don't think so.

ATTORNEY DAVIS: I'm going to show you what has been marked for identification as Exhibit No. 12. Tell the jury what that is, please?

THE WITNESS: It's—it's a sweatshirt.

ATTORNEY DAVIS: What kind of sweatshirt?

THE WITNESS: A blue hoodie. A blue zip-up hoodie.

ATTORNEY DAVIS: Do you recognize that hoodie?

THE WITNESS: I—I guess.

ATTORNEY DAVIS: Is it the same hoodie you saw Elaine Baxter wearing when she snuck out of the cabin to meet Jackson Winter after midnight on the night that he died?

THE WITNESS: It— I don't— I mean, it looks the same. Some of it.

ATTORNEY DAVIS: What about it looks the same?

THE WITNESS: Well, the color, I guess. And the

thumbholes. And it's the same brand and frayed at the pocket in the right place.

ATTORNEY DAVIS: All those characteristics match those of the hoodie you saw Elaine Baxter wearing that night?

THE WITNESS: Yes.

ATTORNEY DAVIS: Then what's different?

THE WITNESS: The— The stains. The stains on it. On the sleeves. Those weren't there before.

ATTORNEY DAVIS: When you saw Miss Baxter wear this hoodie on previous occasions, it did not previously have bloodstains?

THE WITNESS: It— No. It did not.

ATTORNEY DAVIS: And to the best of your knowledge, when Elaine Baxter left the cabin wearing the hoodie to go meet Jackson Winter on the dock the same night that he died, there were no such stains on the hoodie already?

THE WITNESS: No. I mean, that's right.

ATTORNEY DAVIS: Thank you, Kayla. I have no further questions, Your Honor.

November 16

Channel 5 News

"The state rested its case against Elaine Baxter today after an especially dramatic day of testimony. Sixteen-year-old former camper
Kayla Martin, who described herself as Baxter's 'best friend,' served
as a clearly reluctant witness for the prosecution, testifying that she
saw Baxter leave their cabin after midnight during the night of Jackson
Winter's death and return hours later, no longer wearing the infamous
blue hoodie that was recovered days later, splattered with Jackson
Winter's blood.

"During cross-examination, Baxter's lawyer, Michael Desir, made
several attempts to poke holes in Kayla Martin's story, challenging
everything from the time Baxter allegedly returned to the cabin, to
Martin's certainty that Baxter was even wearing the blue hoodie when
she left to meet Winter in the first place, to the closeness of the girls'
relationship. The teenage witness appeared to be fighting back tears
when she told the defense attorney, quote, 'I wish so hard I could tell
you a different story. I really do. I'd give anything for there to be a different end to this. But there isn't.' End quote.

"When the witness left the stand, she appeared to mouth the words
'I'm sorry' in the defendant's direction. Elaine Baxter, who appeared
stone-faced and unresponsive throughout her friend's testimony
against her, turned her head and looked away.

"The defense will call its first witness when the trial resumes tomorrow morning. Elaine Baxter, sources tell us, is currently not expected to
take the stand herself."

November 17

Dear Lainie,

I barely recognized you in the courtroom yesterday.

No, that's not right.

I recognized you immediately, of course. But the blankness of your stare—the indifference in your eyes as you looked straight at me and let my words wash over you—was not the *you* you used to be with me. It was all Teflon. Any pleas I tried to send in your direction bounced right off. Your posture, your expression—you gave nothing away, and you were letting in no one, especially not me. Of all the truly awful things about yesterday, that is what made it a nightmare. The pure and total eradication of *us*.

You're done with me. I know that. Despite your face saying nothing, the message was all too clear. Your complete and total silence has been screaming it at me all along. I didn't want to listen. But I get it now. I do.

If you'd given me just the slightest sign, I don't think I could have gone through with it. So thank you, I guess. In a way, you've made this easier, despite it being so far from what I wanted.

None of this is what I wanted.

Your lawyer is doing a shit job. I wanted to shake him. He's been sowing seeds of doubt, but he hasn't planted a new story. There's nothing for those seeds to grow into. It's a huge mistake.

People need stories. They crave narratives to follow, characters to believe in. Tales to help them understand. They want to be told something beautiful, horrible, strange, or exhilarating—to imagine and feel part of it. Stories get us invested. They make us care. A good story can get a listener so attached, she'll believe it regardless of truth. You taught me that. Give people a few convincing threads and they'll spin the rest themselves.

This story has been woven for us, more tightly than I could have done. I couldn't untangle the knots now if I tried—everyone's too invested in what they want to believe. It's too late to suggest all the things they got wrong.

But this part's right: That night, you snuck out to meet Jackson, alone. You didn't even glance in my direction as you slipped out the screen door, shoes in hand, hoodie on. The next morning, Jackson was dead. That's a nice, clean arc for those who want to see it.

It's the part before that that's murkier, that I'm still reluctant to believe: The part where I told you what Nitin had told me, and everything got thrown off-kilter.

I expected pain when I told you the truth about Jackson. Pain and fury, and some disbelief. Maybe some of your anger would be directed at me—after all, no one thanks the messenger. It's an ugly job, delivering news that hurts. I'd rather have avoided it and spared us both.

That whole afternoon, I tried to talk myself into a way I wouldn't have to tell you. What did it matter if he deceived you for two more days, then broke your heart with the truth in the end? Either way, you'd get crushed. But if I waited, I wouldn't be there to help pick up the pieces—I'd be home and so would you. I couldn't abandon you to go through it alone. Besides, the longer this went on before you learned the full truth, the more humiliated you would be that you hadn't seen it coming. You wouldn't want me to let him keep playing you like that.

Maybe Jackson could lie to your face, but I couldn't. Best friends tell each other hard truths. We say the things no one else will, and we stay close to help break the fall. That's friendship. That's trust.

So I told you. I pulled you aside at campfire that night and repeated what Nitin had said. Light and shadows from the flames danced across your face, and I waited for the shock to register.

Instead, you looked only exhausted.

I was tired by then too—tired of watching you run on this hamster wheel; tired of sharing my best friend with a dirtbag; tired of how different you were around him; and tired, most of all, of him. But that wasn't what you were tired of. You seemed tired of *me*.

That sent me reeling.

I touched your arm, almost to steady myself. To ground us in something real. You blinked, and your expression changed. Exhaustion and annoyance morphed into resignation. You sighed and shook your head, and I wondered if I had misread things.

"Nitin's wrong. He and Jackson don't really hang anymore. I get why he'd assume that, but he doesn't have the full story," you said.

Maybe I should have dropped it, but I couldn't. "I don't think so. He's not the type to just go around saying things. He seemed certain. Maybe you should, um, ask."

"Okay." Your voice was calm and steady.

"Okay, you'll ask him? Ask Jackson?"

You shrugged. "Sure."

His arms snaked around you from behind, and I jumped. "Ask me what?" he said. Over your shoulder, he gave me his signature smirk.

You turned so your lips could meet his. "Nothing," you said, and kissed him again. There were counselors and campers all around, but you didn't care that PDA was prohibited. Two days left—the rules were getting lax.

"Not *nothing*," I said. I was annoyed, I admit it. My tone was a violation of our truce from the past few days. But Jackson had broken the truce first through his deception.

You shot me a glare. *I'm on it*, your look said. *Butt out*. Maybe you planned to catch him off guard with questions later. Maybe you wanted to ask him in private, even though you would tell me everything when it was done. I wanted to be there for it, though. I wanted to be there to keep him honest. He'd already lied and convinced you once. You might fall for more of what you wanted to hear. I wouldn't.

But you were right. This was not my battle to fight, and you had told me you would ask him. I needed to let you do it on your own time, in your own way. I backed off. "You want s'mores?" I asked. "I can get us sticks."

Jackson kissed your neck and you leaned against him. "Don't you have somewhere else to be? Anyone else at all to hang out with?" you said to me.

The words stole my breath. They wrapped around my heart and squeezed, while your acid tone finished the job. If you wanted me to feel worthless and pathetic in that moment, you succeeded. I stumbled backward, as thrown as if you'd shoved me.

You never talked to me that way when Jackson wasn't around. You weren't cruel or dismissive toward anyone, before him. But Jackson made you mean. His "jokes" were designed to cut people down. He was a guy—he could get away with it. He was "being funny" and "just kidding" and "didn't realize" anyone "could be so sensitive" if they showed they were hurt or didn't always laugh along. Boys will be boys, hahaha. And the fact that you were his sort-of girlfriend protected him as much as the double standards did. He was a jerk, but you liked him, and people put up with it because of how much they liked you.

But when his behavior put you on edge, the poison he kept injecting in your veins seeped out and damaged others. I don't think you meant to be that way. You were trying to impress him, not trying to hurt anyone. But the barbs still sliced and stung.

You got away with it, to a point, because people already admired you. You were so fun and magnetic the rest of the time. But it added up. It affected how people saw you by the end, and put them on guard. They didn't trust you. And why should they? You'd hurt them for the sake of a laugh.

That wasn't you. It was a wounded, worn-down version of you with too much to prove.

Knowing that didn't stop the hit from landing when you lashed out at me in that moment. I backed away, apologizing, and tried to catch my breath. I left you alone the rest of the evening.

You were normal toward me that night in the cabin as everyone hung out and got ready for bed. But we didn't get any moments alone together, and when I tried to check in quietly while we were brushing our teeth, you gestured to say, *Not now*.

"Tonight?" I asked, and you shook your head and bent to spit out the toothpaste. So we wouldn't be sneaking out. It was decided.

I swallowed my disappointment with a few handfuls of tap water, and rationalized it was probably so we wouldn't be tired on the last full day. We'd want to sneak out the final night, of course. Maybe we would stay out until dawn, watch the sunrise over the lake, spend every hour we had left together *together*, like how we'd started. Tonight we would sleep, to enable us to end strong. I was okay with that.

We went to bed. I sort of slept, but my brain was too jumpy to rest for long. I kept waking up, checking the time, and getting annoyed that only ten, thirteen, eighteen minutes had passed. As this rate, the night would be endless.

I got more frustrated by my insomnia with every second. The more frustrated I got, the more impossible it was to sleep. Since we weren't sneaking out, being awake was a total waste, and I'd be even more annoyed with myself when I spent our last day completely exhausted. I wanted to scream.

When you climbed down from your bunk, I felt a rush of hope. I thought maybe you'd been lying there sleepless too and decided *fuck it*, we might as well go out. I held still and waited for you to come over and nudge me awake. You didn't even look in my direction.

In one smooth motion, you picked up your shoes, opened the screen door without a sound, and crept outside, into the night. Without me.

Okay, I thought. *Okay*. You were going to meet Jackson. That made sense. You hadn't had the right moment to confront him with the truth, so you'd asked him to meet you at the dock, alone. You would ask him for answers and he'd tell you. It would be done soon. Finally over.

You could have asked me to go with you, to wait for you nearby, but you'd had hours to steel yourself up for this. You knew what was coming. You'd had time to get angry, to get ready for the end. You were going into this breakup with the upper hand this time. You felt strong. You had resolve. You didn't need me there, waiting to help you. You could handle that asshole on your own.

But . . . what if he lost his temper? What if he got cruel? What if he lied again and convinced you, or you lost the nerve to go through with it?

I sat up. You hadn't asked me to go, but you didn't have to. I was your best friend. I should be there. I got up, grabbed the closest sneakers (yours, but my only footwear in sight was flip-flops, and your feet are only a half size bigger), went out the door, slipped on the shoes, and started down the hill toward the water.

The quarter moon slid out from behind the clouds and by the time I passed the last cabin on the girls' side, my eyes had adjusted to the darkness. It was strange being out in the still of night without you. Creepier. The campgrounds seemed empty and huge. Less familiar than when I was with you.

I neared the path to dock and slowed to listen. The leaves rustled and a loon cried, but you and Jackson kept your voices quiet. If I hadn't known you were out there, I would have missed any signs of you entirely. There was only the softest murmur, or was that a moan? I froze, still out of sight, and listened. Nothing.

Then . . . a slight laugh. Was that a slap? No, just the motion of the dock. More nothing. My head buzzed and spun from the strain of my efforts. There weren't any sounds of fighting or distress. There weren't many sounds of anything. This wasn't the scene I'd been expecting.

I stepped away, moved left along the water, on the path toward the boys' cabins. Near the steps of the boathouse, I stopped. A soft lump on the ground that at first I mistook for a cat or raccoon held still, watching, and I watched it back for several seconds, wondering who would move first, before I realized it wasn't an animal—it was your sweatshirt. I picked it up.

The scene flashed before my eyes: you, meeting Jackson here, waiting for him on this step. Standing when he approached. Letting him kiss you. Kissing him back, and running your hands under his T-shirt to feel his warm skin. Letting him unzip your hoodie and push it off your arms. Leaving it where it fell. Lacing your fingers through his and leading him down the path toward the dock, where you could continue what you'd started, and more.

His fingernails running down your back. The arch of your spine. Your lips on his skin. I saw it all.

My stomach turned. You'd been so calm when I told you what Nitin had said. You weren't clinging to disbelief. You believed it completely because you already knew.

I was shaking. Suddenly freezing. I put on your sweatshirt, lifted the hood, and crossed my arms tight against myself. I needed to sit before the realization knocked me over.

You had lied. You lied to me. You lied for Jackson, lied about Jackson. Lied to get me off your case. Lied to push me away. Lied because you had chosen him—lying, cheating, lousy, lazy him—over me. Even though you knew he didn't love you. Even though you knew how much I did.

I felt sick. This had to stop.

I tucked my head between my knees and took deep breaths through my nose, trying to keep the world from spinning, trying to slow my racing heart. With each inhale, I smelled the scent of your hoodie, a mix of campfire and cotton, coconut body wash, the lake, a hint of sweat, and cinnamon gum. I breathed deeper.

I had to save you from him. You would never save yourself. I saw it clearly now: You would go back to him again and again. The cycle would never end. We were too imbalanced, you were too desperate, and as long as Jackson was in the equation, the numbers would never add up right. You had let him come between us once, and you would let it happen again. You were obsessed. You'd lost all sense of yourself with him.

We were past the point where I could reason you out of this. You wouldn't listen. I had to act. I had to figure out a way to shock you out of it and bring you back to yourself. Back to us.

I got up from the steps of the boathouse, went inside. Without turning on the lights or even knowing what I was looking for, my hands found it: the industrial flashlight. The same one kept in every cabin near the first aid kit and fire extinguisher. In case of emergency. I gripped it and went outside.

The flashlight was heavy and sturdy, and I felt calmer just holding it. Something solid. Something useful. Even though I still had no idea what to do with it. I thought maybe I'd go to the dock, shine the flashlight in your faces. Let it blind you and scare you; make you think I was a counselor and you'd been caught.

But that wouldn't go well. You'd made it clear you didn't want me inserting myself in any of this. You'd drawn a line in the sand, with you and Jackson on one side, and me stuck on the other. If I shone the light in your faces, it would only make the dividing line wider. It would only turn you further against me.

It was the next-to-last night of camp and you were choosing him over me, knowing full well he'd only betray you, knowing for sure he was dicking you around. How the fuck had this happened? How the hell was I supposed to stop it?

I shouldn't stand there. If you came back for your sweatshirt, you would see me and think I had followed you. Which I had, but I didn't want it to seem like stalking. That wouldn't end well, either. I had no plan. I moved away from the boathouse and stepped off the path. Leaned my back against a tree trunk. Felt it hold me. Listened to the water. Waited for you to say goodnight.

The lies you had told me weren't you. You only told them because of Jackson. He'd made you need him, made you desperate, through withholding and manipulation. But once you were free of him, the obsession would stop. You would need me again, just like I needed you. There would be no more of anyone misleading anyone. Only friendship. Only trust. You would be yourself again, and we'd both be grateful for it.

There was only one way to save us. I didn't want to. But I would do anything for you.

Anything.

In your right mind, I knew you would do anything for me too.

The seventh rule of crime is: Dance Like You Mean It, a.k.a. Go Hard or Go Home.

If I was going to do it, I had to go all the way.

I would make it look like an accident. No one would be at fault but Jackson. He was always making bad decisions—showing off could lead to poor judgment. He wasn't exactly known for his forethought.

It would be tragic, and we would mourn him.

Together.

It would bring us closer.

Don't you see what this all could have been?

Love,
Kayla

Camper and Counselor Interviews, Statements, and Posts
August 14–November 24

"I hope they lock her up forever. It disgusts me, what she did. Jackson had his whole life ahead of him, and she took that. She just . . . took it. Because, what—he wanted to be with someone else? She didn't get to own and control him? It's disturbing. Really disturbing, that kind of mind-set. I'm sure she thought she'd get away with it too. People like that always do. But not this time. I'm glad. Poor Jackson, getting mixed up in that. Can you imagine? They should lock her up and toss the key, teach everyone like her a lesson."

"It doesn't make sense. Would a girl like Lainie really kill a guy like Jackson, just because he didn't want to be with her? I don't think so. I can't wrap my head around it. It doesn't add up. There has to be more to this story."

"I can't believe I ever envied Jackson and Lainie's relationship. This is so messed up.

"I don't care how heartbroken I was, I would never react by stabbing the person or pushing them off a cliff, or poisoning their omelet or whatever. I definitely wouldn't bash them over the head with whatever she used to kill him. They never found the murder weapon, right? That's messed up too. This is real and it happened with people I actually know and spent time with and that's just . . .

"I don't want to date *anyone* now. I keep looking at people I've known for years and thinking, *Would* you *bash someone's skull in if they dumped you?* How do you know? Like, how do you know if a person's safe? I might be overreacting or unreasonable or whatever, but really: Who can you trust?"

November 20

Now Today

ELAINE BAXTER'S FATE NOW RESTS IN THE HANDS OF
the jury. After two days of testimony from witnesses for the
defense—including fellow campers who described the deceased,
Jackson Winter, as "a risk-taker" who "seemed to consider himself
invincible"; a cabinmate who said she "thought" Baxter "might" have
returned to their cabin much earlier during the night in question than
a prosecution witness previously testified; and two counselors who
each described seeing Baxter appear "legitimately shocked" and
"distraught," "nearly hysterical with grief as the reality sank in," and
seeming "to have no idea what had happened" on the morning Winter's body was discovered—Elaine Baxter waived her own right to
testify on Thursday afternoon, as legal experts had predicted, and the
defense rested its case.

On her way out of the courthouse, Baxter addressed reporters for
the first time in a seemingly unplanned outburst. Breaking away from
her lawyer, who usually ushers Baxter quickly past the many cameras
and microphones her trial has attracted, Baxter said, "I never hurt
anyone. I would never hurt Jackson. There's probably nothing I can
say to make you believe me, but I'm innocent. I am innocent. People
think what they want to think, but I didn't do it. He was my friend. The
last time I saw him, he was alive. He was alive, and I miss him. I miss
him so much. Everyone who thinks I did this is wrong." She did not
answer follow-up questions.

On Friday morning, the prosecution and defense delivered their closing statements, and Judge Rodriguez gave final instructions to the jurors and released them to the task of deliberations.

Reporters and spectators gathered outside the courtroom—and, especially, Jackson Winter's parents and other family members—now must wait, however long it takes for the jury to reach their verdict. The question in everyone's mind is, which version of Elaine Baxter will the jurors find most compelling: the scorned ex-girlfriend with a history of blatant lies and deceit, who turned to violence when her jealousy peaked; or the misunderstood and unfairly maligned girl who lost a close friend in this tragedy made doubly tragic by the fact of her being falsely accused? We won't know until the verdict is delivered.

November 24

Dear Jackson,

Lainie was convicted of your murder today. They found her guilty of wrongfully and intentionally causing your death, and she'll be sentenced to anywhere from fifteen years to life, at a hearing next month. I thought you'd want to know.

Your family gets closure just in time for Thanksgiving, and I guess I do too, in a way, though there are parts of this wound that will never heal. Perhaps you can relate, haha.

When I testified (I didn't want to, but they don't exactly make it optional), I promised to tell the truth, the whole truth, and nothing but the truth, and I did that. Well, I mostly told the truth. As the king of broken promises and convenient half-truths, you can forgive me for that, right?

Good boy.

It's weird to snark at you like usual and have you unable to snark back. It is indescribably weird being at the center of all this, yet also essentially irrelevant now. But I'm not the one who excluded me first. Lainie did that. She did it because of you.

Do you even know what really happened that night? Or was it too fast, too unexpected, too painful to process before you died? We were friends of a sort, once upon a time, and I think you deserve to know the story of your own death. So I'll tell it to you, just this once. Maybe I'll print the letter and burn it so the ashes and fumes can waft into your consciousness, if you still have one—that or a soul or whatever. I don't think I believe in an afterlife, but if you're in one, I hope it's fine. I don't need you to rot in hell for eternity. I'm not a monster.

I'm just a girl who couldn't stand to lose her best friend.

I lost her anyway. But at least you lost her too. You're the only one of the three of us who got what was deserved.

You get why you deserved it, right? I'd like to think you understand that. Though I guess if you had an ounce of self-awareness, or the teeniest bit of empathy for the needs of other people, we wouldn't exactly be in this place. If you could have seen Lainie for who she was—if you appreciated even a fraction of how beautiful and brilliant and vulnerable and strong and anxious and gutsy and ugly and wonderful and imperfect and *Lainie-ish* she could be—then none of this would have happened. Because if she were a person to you—a real, full person—you wouldn't have treated her the way you did. You wouldn't have yanked her around and played with her emotions like a cat batting a ball of string.

It was a game to you. She was a challenge. You saw her as a pretty, shiny, impressive thing, and you wanted to win her. You wanted to win her so you could pull her down off the pedestal you'd placed her on. You wanted to bring her to the edge and watch her fall, because your ego couldn't stand to see her above you.

She didn't ask to be put on that pedestal, but when you yanked, she had to scramble to stay up. Because she liked you. She really did. And though you didn't want her existing above you, you couldn't handle her being real and on the ground like a normal, actual human, either. You needed her to be an idea of a girl—hot, messy, unattainable. Unattainable to everyone but you.

She wasn't a toy or a trophy for you to acquire and discard. *You* were the disposable one, Jackson. That's what we proved in the end.

She let you do it, though. You thought it was funny to rile her up, to stoke her emotions by pretending you couldn't see them, and she played her part, like a dancing bear when the music starts. (Do you know how they train those bears? They heat the floor until it's burning hot, and the bears dance to save their feet from sizzling. When the music plays again, it triggers the memory of the pain, and that's enough to make them dance again. Fucked up, right?) She bent and contorted, danced away and came back, trying to be the idea of a girl you saw in her.

It was obvious you didn't see *her* at all. You didn't want to. You just wanted a power trip. And you got one. Was it fun? Was it worth it?

Lainie was real to me. She was real, and she was everything. I'd never had a friend like that. Not even close. I may never have one again.

You didn't care if you hurt her, but *I* cared. You didn't care what she needed, but *I* did. You didn't care about what was good for her, or what she wanted, or what you damaged. You only cared about yourself. And you wore her down, eroded her self-worth, until you were all she cared about too.

She was ready to give up everything for you, even me. I wouldn't let her. I refused to let you destroy us. I would end this twisted dance.

If anyone told me at the start of summer I would kill someone by the end, I'd have assumed they were a lousy fortune-teller, in need of better meds, and deeply, deeply confused about what I'm capable of. I'm still surprised I had it in me, to be honest. Surprised and kind of proud. I was dreading the whole thing, every millisecond leading up to it, but when I finally stepped out from behind that tree and slammed the flashlight into your head, it hit your skull with the kind of *thunk* I can only describe as satisfying. My arms vibrated from the force of the impact, and you fell to the ground, eyes wide-open, but clearly unconscious. I pushed you over with my foot and hit you again for good measure. The second hit broke the skin—a small gash, but still bleeding—and I knew I needed to move you quickly so there wouldn't be a trail of blood.

I pulled off your sneakers, shorts, and shirt (thanks for wearing a button-down that night—it would have been tough to get a T-shirt off without it touching the blood that matted your hair). You'd have dived in fully naked, of course, but I couldn't bring myself to remove your underwear. It wasn't for your sake, please understand. I left them on to preserve *my* dignity. I was sick of seeing too much of you all summer long. I didn't need your dick flopping around in my mental image bank.

I hefted you by sliding one arm beneath each of your armpits, and dragged you down the bank. This was harder than it sounds, by the way—you were scrawny, and I'm not weak, but it's not easy dragging close to six feet of dead weight even a short distance. I kicked off my shoes, lowered you into the water, and held you there, face-down, hoping that drowning wouldn't wake you. I couldn't breathe until I was certain you weren't, either. You made it clear by sinking. (I always think of dead bodies as floating, but I looked it up after on a school computer, and you were normal: Corpses sink when the air in their lungs is replaced with water. They only pop back up later, when decomposition fills the body with gas. Neat, huh? If you'd been dead, not just unconscious, when we got to the lake, you'd have stayed on the surface.)

I left you in the shallow water—I figured dead bodies can drift, so that was realistic, and moving you around might create suspicious evidence—and did my best to make the ground between the lake and the trail look like no one had been dragged over it recently. I was lucky there were all those long pine needles around. Camp Cavanick really is the best place ever.

I took your clothes and shoes to the dock and left them there in a messy pile, like you would have before you dived in. The flashlight I'd used for your head wounds I threw as far into the lake as I could, and listened for the *plop* as it went under. (That wasn't a surprise. I knew flashlights sink.)

I went back to the scene of the crime to make sure nothing looked amiss, then returned up the hill to my cabin. It was strange walking back in the darkness by myself, but less strange than it had been walking down there. I didn't like sneaking out without Lainie. The night was ours. It wasn't right being out in it alone. That wasn't how things should be—but it would be different from now on.

The crickets chirped and the breeze was soft, and I felt calm and okay. Things would be better now.

In the morning, you would be missing. Once they found you, there would be shock, then sadness, disbelief, mourning. We would remember the good with the bad—how stubborn you could be, and infuriatingly overconfident. How quick you were to tease and slow to form grudges, since you never took anything seriously. Your habit of pushing boundaries and need to show off, and the risks those caused you to take. Risks like sneaking out after midnight. Risks like diving into shallow water. Risks like laughing off things other people knew to take seriously.

We would bury you, but keep the best memories. Our shared loss would bring Lainie and me closer—as would our shared relief. You would rest in peace after your tragic accident. And we would move on.

At the door to the cabin, I realized my one mistake. I was still wearing Lainie's hoodie, which I'd found on the ground where she'd left it earlier, when she took it off for you. She must have forgotten to retrieve it later, but what if in the morning she remembered? Or what if someone else got to it first? I couldn't leave it where I'd found it—that would suggest to the next finder she was with you. But if I took it off in our cabin, hung it up on the hooks by the door, she might realize it hadn't been there all night and connect the dots to how it made its way back. Both risks seemed too big to take.

I looked down and saw the choice had been made for me. I couldn't leave it where I'd found it or return it to where it belonged. It had your blood on the sleeves. Blood that definitely wouldn't be there if you had died from a risky dive, all alone.

I peeled it off and hid it beneath the cabin steps. There would be time in the morning to find a better spot for it. For now, I needed to crawl into bed and sleep.

And I did. I slept so well, knowing you were gone. I'd done what

I had to, because that's the kind of friend I am. The kind who will fight for what matters and have no regrets.

That's it. That's the story. It's a good one, right?

All's well that ends well, but the end of this one got twisted.

It got all turned around, and she let it. She refused to remember what's true.

Nobody else knows how it should have been.

Nobody knows but you.

Kayla

November 28

Dear Lainie,

We need to talk about the morning after. About how when news broke that Jackson was gone, you broke too. And then you let it break us. You *used* it to break us, when it was supposed to do the exact opposite. I've been turning this around in my head for months, the mental Rubik's Cube of what went down. I don't think it will ever make sense.

If you could live it all again today, would you choose differently? I would.

I would kill Jackson much, much sooner.

You were crabby that morning, and moving slowly—probably tired from your excursion with Jackson the night before, and feeling down about it being the last full day of camp. Lots of people were sad about that. There was an overall gloomy mood in the mess hall, and you stayed quieter than usual, like you needed to really focus on pushing around the scrambled eggs and soggy Froot Loops on your tray. I jumped in to fill the space with chatter, then tried to damp myself down so I wouldn't annoy you. (When Adele acts that way, too chipper in the early morning, I want to slosh my orange juice in her face, so I get it. But moms are supposed to get on our nerves. Best friends aren't.) You weren't listening to me anyway. You were watching over my shoulder for Jackson to appear, and getting crankier by the second when he didn't. Maybe things hadn't been all copacetic between you two last night after all.

"Hey," I said, to pull you out of it. "You okay?"

You sighed and dragged your fork through the eggs you hadn't tasted. "Yeah. Just . . . distracted. Sorry. What were you saying about sled dogs?"

"What?" I laughed, and you laughed too. I hadn't said anything about sled dogs. "Now who's random?" I teased. You smiled. We were good.

You pushed your tray away. "Let's skip out on packing and swim across the lake."

"To the island?" I said.

"Yeah! I always wanted to do that." You'd never mentioned it before, and I wasn't sure we could actually make it (let alone make it back), but your eyes had the spark of a hatching plan—a plan for you and me—so I was in.

"What are they going to do, kick us out on the last day? They don't need another bucket of garlic peeled," you said. Your sulkiness was gone and your enthusiasm contagious, and I honestly forgot about what (or who) was already in the lake that might stop us, until I saw Hot Hot Raúl, the paddleboard instructor, run across the mess hall to find Director Skip. Raúl spoke rapidly and quietly into the director's ear, motioning wildly, and Skip rose from his seat, his eyes cartoonishly wide. The two of them rushed out a side door, and the other adults at the table looked at one another and shrugged. I glanced around. Most of the room hadn't noticed.

My heartbeat thudded in my ears. It was happening.

I reached for my juice glass and lifted my chin toward the door through which they'd left. "I guess the lake is on fire," I said.

You rolled your eyes. "Yeah, right. Or Hot Hot Raúl wants to snitch on some turtles they caught mating under the boathouse." Raúl was simmering hot, but a stickler for rules, and you never forgave them for being strict about PDA and life vests. Their stubbornness crimped your style.

I wondered how Jackson's body had looked when Raúl found it. Was it still submerged? Had it drifted from where I'd left it, or gotten bloated? How long did corpses take to start deteriorating in water? Did fish bite them? I'd been fine without a phone all summer, but now my fingers itched for Google. Maybe because I couldn't bounce those questions off you.

(I would tell you everything someday, but the less you knew then, the better. I kept it to myself to protect you.

Ugh. I really was naïve.)

We heard the ambulance before we saw it. It drove straight to the lake, lights flashing, a county police car seconds behind it. We stood and surged toward the commotion with everyone else, but a second cop car pulled up and parked near the mess hall. Two officers jumped out and corralled the bewildered-seeming counselors who weren't already down by the lake to step up and do some crowd control. We were ordered to stay in the mess hall or on its patio, where of course everyone squeezed to look. The cops continued down to the lakefront on foot, and I stood on tiptoe to see the swarm of people already making a mess of what they didn't seem to realize was a crime scene. *Good.*

"Jackson will be sorry he missed this," you said, seeming to take some satisfaction from the sentiment. I wondered again if you'd ended last night on an off note or just wanted him taught a lesson for skipping breakfast.

"You guys okay still?" I asked, and you shrugged a little.

"Mostly." You moved away to get a better view and I followed, though it was clear that was the most I'd be getting out of you for the moment. Which was fine. We'd have all the time in the world to rehash the subject of Jackson. You would tell me everything that happened that night and more, when you were ready—once his hold on you was lifted and you'd come back to me. Or so I thought.

The ambulance came back up the hill, moving slower this time. You leaned forward. "What does it mean when the lights flash but there's no siren?" you asked.

"I think that it's not an emergency? Like, not urgent?" I guessed.

"Oh." You looked disappointed. "Sprained ankle or something. Figures." Though Nurse Phil had taken care of those all summer.

I shrugged. "Or maybe the person's already dead."

You laughed and hooked your arm through mine. "I want Froot Loops," you said. So we went back in for second breakfast, and this time you actually ate yours.

People remembered that later, but with the timing wrong— readjusted to make you a villain. I heard Maddie mention it online: how everyone was out there worried sick about what happened to Jackson, and you were grinning and eating cereal. "Heartless bitch," I think she called you. Like she hadn't been one of your devoted groupies all summer.

The next few hours passed slowly, but I was so hyped up, they're a blur in my memory. Was there an announcement about it being

Jackson, or just a rumor that quickly spread? It felt like no one knew, then everyone knew, but what we knew was wrong and constantly changing.

He was dead on arrival, then alive but badly injured. Then not alive, then close to death, then brain-dead but on life support, then conscious and asking for his girlfriend (the real one, then you), then comatose and not expected to make it. Every rumor seemed official yet completely false. It was exhausting.

They kept us in the mess hall forever, but we were back in our cabins forever too, and I can't remember how or when we got there. They let us have our phones out so parents could text us. We were supposed to pack, but no one did, yet the drawers got emptied and duffels and backpacks stuffed, so we must have gone through the motions at some point. The police and Director Skip asked to speak to us, one by one—you were first, and I tried to go with you, but you shook your head and the counselors wouldn't let me—but we didn't know anything yet, so how could we answer their questions? When did they answer ours? I can't remember. The specifics go in and out of focus.

Here's what I do remember, vividly, though the sequence is jumbled: How when I moved close to comfort you, you pushed me away. How I was there for you to confide in, but you shut down and shut me out. I was there for you like I always am—always will be—and you made it clear you didn't want me. You wanted no one but him.

Even once he was dead, you chose Jackson over me. I will never get over that. Never.

I truly thought you would turn to me. That once the shock sank in and your daze turned to distress, you would need me to steady and support you. I wanted to be the one to wipe your tears and calm your grief. To make you see this would all be okay—that maybe, in the end, it would even be good. I would help you remember you didn't need him. That actually, he was kind of a shit to you. That you still and always had me.

You never gave me the chance. You were so focused on him, you could only think of yourself. You closed me out in a way that dismissed the idea I might have feelings about Jackson's death too, that anyone might. It was all about you. *Your* loss. You and him. Even though I'd ended that.

I'd truly thought his death would break the spell and bring you back to me, like Sleeping Beauty in reverse: I would prick your finger and wake you from this trance. Open your eyes to reality. Free you from Jackson's hold. Undo the poison of his kiss.

But you didn't want to be free of him. If anything, you got worse. You were too upset to see clearly.

It sent me reeling.

I tried to help you refocus and understand how you might need me. To remind you I was on your side. "I'll tell them I was with you," I said. Was it before the first time you spoke to the cops, or after? I think after. You must have already been questioned once and I was waiting my turn. "I'll say we all snuck out, and you and I went to the cabin together after saying goodnight on the dock. We weren't there when he dove in. I'll be your alibi."

"What?" You'd been calm—distraught but calm, all emotions boxed in—but my words jarred you out of it. Finally, some real feelings seeped out. You got hysterical.

"Go away. I don't need you to lie for me. I don't need you to do anything except leave me alone for once. I don't want a fucking alibi. I want Jackson back. What the hell is wrong with you?"

I wrapped my arms around your shoulders, ready to absorb your anger and tears. You shoved me away.

"Can't you take a fucking hint and leave me alone for just one second? Jackson is dead. I'll never see him again."

"I know. It's okay," I said.

"It's not okay!" you screamed. I tried to hug you again. You pushed. "Get off! God, you're so obsessed with me."

I stumbled backward, and understood: It was too late. I was too late. The plan wasn't going to bring you back to me. I should have found a way to get rid of him sooner.

This was his fault. You and he were the opposite of you and me. We always brought out the best in each other. With you, I was ten times better than I could be on my own. My world and my heart were fuller, bolder, more alive, because of everything you opened up in me. And our friendship had that effect on you too. I knew it did because I'd seen, with Jackson, who you were without me. You needed me. I was certain of that. The only one who couldn't see it was you.

That's when I decided, I think. If you'd shown the slightest remorse, the tiniest hint that deep down, you knew you didn't mean it, were only lashing out because you were sad and confused and embarrassed you'd let him get to your head—regretful you'd ever lied to me—I'd have forgiven you immediately, and let everything go according to plan.

His death could have been a tragic accident. It was *supposed* to be an accident—a thoughtless dive by a reckless kid, which ended in horrible disaster. No one at fault but the deceased, and who can blame a cocky teenager for not grasping his own mortality? He should have been fine, but these things happen. So sad.

The cops were ready to see it that way, and my plan was to let that stand. But you ruined it. You ruined it by turning on me. Turning me away. By caring more about Jackson—even dead Jackson—than you cared about our friendship.

I'd been willing to do anything to fight for us. You wouldn't save yourself from him, so I did. I did that for you. But I wasn't willing to do what you were asking of me next. I wouldn't let you push me away forever, and just go.

I could never move on from losing you, and I would not let you move on from me. I would find another way to fight for us, and stop you from walking away.

All summer I'd been the Charlotte to your Wilbur, supporting you and rescuing you and helping you shine. Asking for nothing in return but the friendship you had offered. It was enough—more than enough—but now suddenly you had withdrawn it.

You were taking me for granted. You'd forgotten you ever loved me, forgotten I'd helped you survive. You denied that you could need me. You denied I was your friend. So I sat in my web and thought and thought, and realized what I had to do. I began to weave. And the message I spun was: Eat her.

It was easy. Easier than I'd imagined—it only took a few strings. Though in retrospect, the ease makes sense.

Remember when I said it's always the boyfriend? That's true, but what's even more true is this: It doesn't matter who did it. In real life, no one investigates these things like they do in the movies—detectives working around the clock for weeks on one case, laser-focused and determined to leave no stone unturned. No police force has time for that.

The cops look for the strongest, most obvious leads, get an idea of what they think happened, and build a case to prove it's true. Once they narrow in on a top suspect, they find the evidence that supports their theory. Arrest the person and move on. Any true-crime aficionado has seen it play out a hundred times. These small-town cops, you never know what they'll get in their heads and run with. They only need a believable story, not a perfect one. And when it came to planting stories, I learned from the master.

I didn't tell them your secrets. I am not that kind of friend. But I told them your lie. You *did* sneak out that night, and hadn't told them. That was enough to cast suspicion in your direction. It suggested a story that people could believe in. They filled in the details themselves.

Once the story was set in motion, even you couldn't stop it. Though honestly, I feel like you barely tried. Maybe deep down you felt guilty about it after all, and decided to pay your penance. Or maybe you stayed in denial about the seriousness of this too, and never believed a jury might convict you.

It's such a waste. None of this needed to happen. It could have turned out so differently.

I wasn't angry when I killed Jackson. I was sad—deeply sad, for both of us, that it had come to this. That you were so deluded and entranced. And I wasn't angry when I told the cops what little they needed to hear. I was resigned. And regretful. But I hoped it was still reversible. That you would come around and give me a sign you were ready for another chance.

Deep down, I guess I'm still waiting for that.

Dr. Rita has helped me see I idealized you sometimes, and still do. That although you were often a good, true friend—a best friend—you could also be selfish. You used me. You weren't always there for me the way I was there for you. I deserved to be treated better than that.

But I forgive you. I still love you. I don't know if there will ever be a time when our friendship can be rebuilt, when I'll write letters I'll actually send. Call you. Visit. A time when you'll come back to me—maybe even be grateful for what I did. But I can hope.

It would be different, of course. The end of camp made it inevitable that our friendship would change. But we could be good still. I know we could. And wouldn't it make a better story that way?

I won't be going back to Camp Cavanick next summer. I heard they're closed indefinitely and might get sued by Jackson's family and other campers' too, for negligence, wrongful death, and emotional distress. I read that camps have insurance to cover the cost of things like this, but no one will send their precious kids there now anyhow. In a few summers, they can open again under a new name.

In some ways I like that it won't go on without us. That seems right. In other ways it feels sad, though obviously it's not the biggest tragedy in all of this. Dina had a summer job scooping ice cream at a fancy shoppe, and they think the place would hire me too. That might be fun. It's a ways away, though. I don't have to decide anything at the moment.

For now I'm just adjusting to the trial being over and the reality that life goes on. My brother came home from college this week (he leaves again tomorrow), and Thanksgiving was good. I helped Peter bake the pies (he's extraordinary at that too, especially chocolate pecan and pear ginger), and Adele didn't invite as many misfits as she usually does, I think to keep me from feeling gawked at. My notoriety as your friend peaked again after I testified, but Dina and Ian have been protective, and we think it will die down soon.

Adele and Peter came into my room the other night and sat on the edge of my bed like I'm five years old and still need tucking in. "We just wanted you to know how proud of you we are," Adele said. She smoothed the covers, and Peter nodded.

"We know nothing about this has been easy or fun, and we have nothing but admiration for the way you've handled it," he said. "You're amazing."

That was nice. My parents can be annoying and clueless, but they always have my back, and I know I'm lucky that way. I do appreciate them, even if it's my job to not show it. If I had parents like yours, things would be a lot harder. I recognize my privilege, as Dina likes to say.

Anyway. I've got to text Dina back to let them know what time I'm coming over. We might go to the mall to start holiday shopping, but more likely we'll just hang at their place and watch movies and talk. I like it there. Their dad makes great popcorn.

But I want you to know you still haven't been replaced. You never will be, okay? I'll always miss you. I'll never forget.

And I will never forgive Jackson for what he did to us. Never. Some people may think justice has been served, but there's no justice in all this. Real justice would be you and me, together again, like the way things were before him.

But that's impossible. So here we are.

Maybe that's the last rule of crime: You Can Never Go Back, So Move Forward.

I hope moving forward brings you back to me, eventually.

I'll still be here.

You're still my best friend.

I would do anything for you.

For us.

Anything.

Love,
Kayla

ACKNOWLEDGMENTS

Much love to my editor, Rosemary Brosnan, for the ways she supports, shapes, challenges, and champions me as a writer. Thank you to everyone at HarperCollins who lends their time and talents to my books, including Courtney Stevenson, Molly Fehr, Liz Byer, Caitlin Lonning, Sabrina Aballe, Suzanne Murphy, and the marketing, sales, and subrights teams. Thanks to Brenna Franzitta for her careful eye, and Hokyoung Kim for the gorgeous cover art. Thank you to my agent, Michael Bourret, for balancing it all with grace and aplomb.

I'm grateful to the friends (writer and non) who have shared their secrets and listened to mine. Extra hugs to Lauren Strasnick, who gave me key feedback on so many things, including an early draft of this book. Thank you Emily X.R. Pan, Terra Elan McVoy, Robin Wasserman, Amy Jo Burns, Alex Arnold, Corey Ann Haydu, Claire Legrand, Terry J. Benton, David Levithan, Deb Caletti, Alison Cherry, Kit Frick, Maxine Kaplan, Bree Barton, Sarah Nicole Smetana, Tiff Liao, and Christa Desir, for crucial conversations along the way.

A special shout-out to the summer friends who burned candles with me on the dock; exchanged letters, ideas, and mixtapes; and saw and shaped who I am. Ongoing love to Andy, Max, Sulaiman, Abby, Giles, Nora, Jess, and Jo. A wink of thanks to Lainie, Jascha, Nitin, Phil, and others whose names I borrowed for this story.

Love and thanks to Nono, writer of letters; Nini, keeper of secrets; and Mama, Ati, Jeremy, Erika, Anna, Sophia, Jeff, and Arugula. How lucky I am to have you.